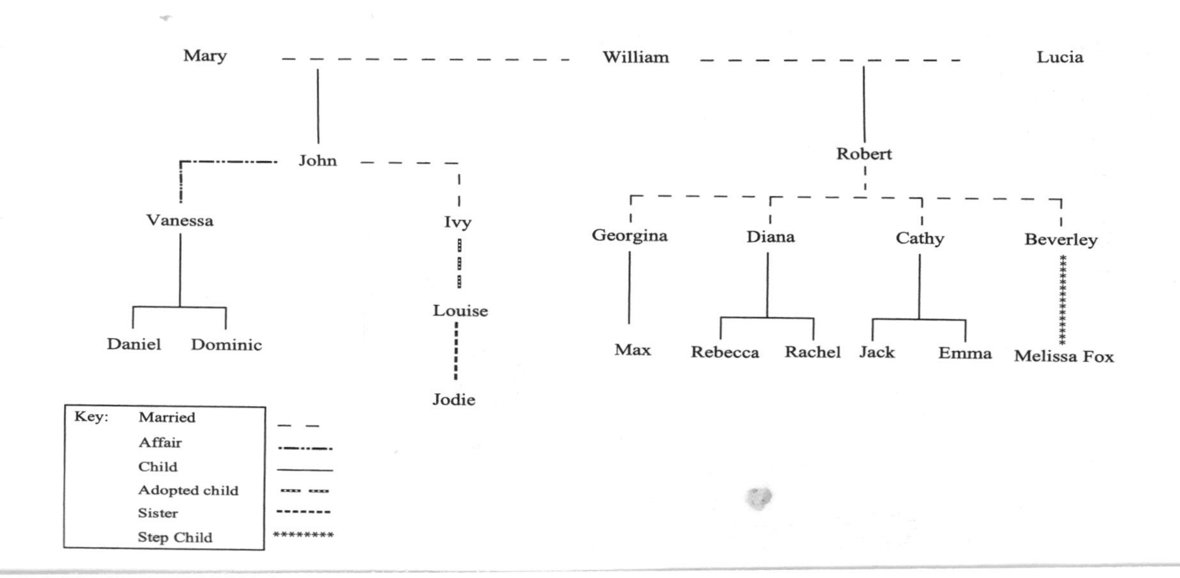

Mary
William
Lucia
John
Robert
Vanessa
Ivy
Georgina
Diana
Cathy
Beverley
Daniel
Dominic
Louise
Max
Rebecca
Rachel
Jack
Emma
Melissa Fox
Jodie
Key:
Married
Affair
Child
Adopted child
Sister
Step Child
****

WITHDRAWN
FROM STOCK

KU-366-204

THE BRIDES OF BELLA LUC

A family torn apart by secrets, reunited by m

When William Valentine returned from the
as a testament to his love for his beautiful Ita
wife Lucia, he opened the first Bella Lucia rest
in London. The future looked bright, and Willi
had, he thought, the perfect family.

Now William is nearly ninety, and not long fo
this world, but he has three top London restauran
with prime spots throughout Knightsbridge and th
West End. He has two sons, John and Robert,
and grown-up grandchildren on both sides
of the Atlantic who are poised to take this
small gastronomic success story into the
twenty-first century.

But when William dies, and the family fight to
control the destiny of the Bella Lucia business,
they discover a multitude of long-buried secrets,
scandals, the threat of financial ruin—
and ultimately two great loves they hadn't
even dreamt of: the love of a lifelong partner—
and the love of a family reunited…

This month, curl up and fall in love
with gorgeous Daniel Valentine in…

***Married Under the Mistletoe* by Linda Goodnight**

MARRIED UNDER THE MISTLETOE

BY

LINDA GOODNIGHT

First published in Great Britain 2006
Harlequin Mills & Boon Limited,
Eton House, 18-24 Paradise Road, Richmond, Surrey TW9 1SR

Special thanks and acknowledgement are given to Linda Goodnight for her contribution to *The Brides of Bella Lucia* series.

ISBN-13: 978 0 263 19239 1
ISBN-10: 0 263 19239 3

Set in Times Roman 10½ on 12½ pt
07-0906-42998

Printed and bound in Great Britain
by Antony Rowe Ltd, Chippenham, Wiltshire

THE BRIDES OF BELLA LUCIA

A family torn apart by secrets, reunited by marriage

First there was double the excitement as we met twins Rebecca and Rachel Valentine

Having the Frenchman's Baby—Rebecca Winters
Coming Home to the Cowboy—Patricia Thayer

Then we joined Emma Valentine as she got a royal welcome this September

The Rebel Prince—Raye Morgan

There was a trip to the Outback to meet Louise Valentine's long-lost sister Jodie

Wanted: Outback Wife—Ally Blake

Now, on these cold November nights, catch up with newcomer Daniel Valentine

Married Under the Mistletoe—Linda Goodnight

Snuggle up with sexy Jack Valentine over Christmas

Crazy About the Boss—Teresa Southwick

In the New Year join Melissa as she heads off to a desert kingdom

The Nanny and the Sheikh—Barbara McMahon

And don't miss the thrilling end to the Valentine saga in February

The Valentine Bride—Liz Fielding

To the children of Gorlovka Hope Orphanage in Ukraine, who may never read the book but who will benefit from its proceeds. My prayers are with you.

CHAPTER ONE

IN HIS wildest fantasies, if he were given to such things, Daniel Stephens had never expected to be here, doing this.

He shifted the heavy canvas duffel bag from his shoulder to the pavement in front of the beautiful, light-washed building, slicked back a damp clutch of hair and gazed up at the Knightsbridge Bella Lucia Restaurant.

London pulsed around him, the genteel hum of the élite, the roar of buses, the swirling, thick moisture of a damp October night, all both familiar and foreign after so many years away.

This was his birth family's restaurant. One of three, if he understood correctly. Fabulously successful. Exclusive. Expensive.

His nostrils flared. Outward façades never impressed him much. To his way of thinking most were lies, like his own childhood, covering a multitude of sins. But he had to admit, the Valentine family had style.

A chic woman stepped out of a taxicab beside him, tucked her designer bag beneath her arm, and sailed past without a glance to enter the glass double-doors of the restaurant. Soft jazz wafted out briefly, then was sucked back inside as the doors vacuumed shut.

Daniel had blood here. Blood that hadn't claimed him or his twin until now when it no longer hurt so much to have no father, no extended family, no one to care. Now his father wanted him. Or so he said. People like John Valentine generally hid ulterior motives. If Daniel waited around awhile, he'd find out what his father was really after.

The notion of claiming John Valentine as father still rankled as much as Mrs Valentine's demand for a DNA test to prove it. He'd refused her request during his brief visit a week and a half ago and, furious, had returned to the familiar call of Africa. But his twin brother Dominic had obliged, proving once and for all that the father who had abandoned them before birth was a rich and respected man.

Now that his troublesome temper had cooled and he'd thought the matter over, Daniel was back. Not that he wanted anything from the family he didn't know or trust. Not at all. But he did want something he couldn't get in Africa. Money. Lots and lots of money.

But first, he needed a place to live. His father—and he used the word loosely—had all but insisted he stay here in the flat above the Knightsbridge restaurant.

Light rain patted against his cheeks. His lips twitched an ironic smile. Water. The most precious commodity on earth. One so abundant here in his native country and so desperately scarce in his adopted one. He'd spent his entire career trying to rectify that problem, but project funds always ran short at the worst possible times. Now he was determined to use his skills and contacts in the UK to change all that. Life's inequities had always bothered him.

He lifted the heavy duffel bag back onto his shoulder. Might as well go up. Introduce himself to the American restaurant manager who had somehow been persuaded to share her lodging with him. He still wondered how John had worked that one out, but the old man had assured him that the woman was not only in agreement but was delighted with the arrangement. After all, the flat was large and roomy and there was some sort of problem in the restaurant that might make a woman alone uneasy. He hadn't added, though Daniel was no fool, that the flat also belonged to the Valentine family and that Miss Stephanie Ellison had no real choice in the matter.

If not for his determination to sink every shilling he had into the new business and ultimately into the Ethiopian water project, he might have felt badly about intruding upon the restaurant manager. He might have. But he didn't.

Obsessing. Stephanie Ellison was obsessing. And she had to get a handle on it fast. She glanced at the stylish pewter clock above the sofa. Five minutes.

"Oh, Lord."

The pressure against her temples intensified.

She paced from one side of her flat to the other, stopping to straighten every piece of framed art, two fresh flower arrangements and a pewter bowl of vanilla potpourri. All useless, obsessive gestures.

The living room, like every other room in the luxury Knightsbridge flat, was immaculate. And why not? She had cleaned, re-cleaned, and triple-cleaned today. Even the cans in the kitchen cupboards were organized into groups according to the alphabet.

And yet the throb in her temple grew louder and her gut knotted as if something was out of order.

Something *was* out of order. Seriously out of order.

"But I can do this." She paced across the white-tiled floor and down the hall to her bedroom to assess her appearance—again. "Oh, why did John put me in this situation?"

Especially now, with the problems in the restaurant. Until the missing money was recovered, Stephanie needed to concentrate her attention there. After all, as manager she was ultimately responsible. But thanks to her employer, she had to deal with an even more dreaded scenario. An unwanted *male* flatmate.

A shudder rippled through her.

John Valentine had no way of knowing that thrusting his son upon her as a temporary roommate had the power to push her over the edge. John, like everyone else, knew nothing of the hidden shame that caused her to keep people at arm's length.

Oh, she was friendly enough. She'd learned from a master to put on a smile, keep her mouth shut, and play the game so that the world at large believed the masquerade instead of the truth.

That was why she'd never taken on a roommate. Brief visits by girlfriends such as Rebecca Valentine, yes. But a roommate? Never. Having someone invade her space for a few days was bad enough. A roommate was sheer terror.

Anyone who got too close might discover the truth. And she couldn't even face that herself.

Since hiring her a year ago as manager of the exclusive Knightsbridge restaurant, the Valentine family had given her carte blanche in remodeling and running the Bella Lucia. They'd even indulged her penchant for contemporary art décor. Her boss seldom interfered. Which was exactly why she hadn't been able to say no when he'd asked her to house the son who'd spent years doing charity work in Africa.

She chewed on that, allowing a seed of hope that Daniel Stephens was as noble as his work implied. From her boss's enthusiastic description, Daniel was one minor step below sainthood.

She laughed, though the sound was as humorless as the hammering in her head.

"A saint. Sure, he is. Like all men."

One other thing worried her. Actually, a lot of other things worried her. But in her flummoxed state, she'd failed to ask how long Daniel would be staying. With all her heart, she hoped not long. There was too much at stake to have him here indefinitely.

She swiveled around backwards, twisting her head to look at the slim, smooth line of her pale green dress. Everything was covered. Nothing showed. But she'd have to be extra careful with a flatmate lurking about. She hated that. Hated worrying that someone would discover the secret she kept hidden away beneath designer labels.

Someone tapped softly at the door.

Stephanie jumped, then gritted her teeth in frustration. She would not, could not, let anxiety take over. The willowy redhead staring back from the mirrored tub enclosure looked in complete control, unruffled, and well groomed. Good. As long as the outside appeared in control, let the inside rage.

She smoothed newly manicured hands down the soft, flowing skirt, realigned the toiletries on the counter for the third time, and went to greet her boss's son.

One look at the big, dark, wild-looking man filling up her foyer and Stephanie's heart slammed against her ribcage. The throbbing in her head intensified. Fight or flight kicked into high gear. Escape lay past him and down the elevator to the restaurant below. She had little choice but to stand and fight.

There had to be a mistake. This could not be Daniel. Mr Valentine had called him a boy, and, even though she had fully expected a grown man, she hadn't expected this…this…barbarian!

"My boy," John had said with an indulgent chuckle. "He's a tad rough around the edges. Too much time abroad living without the amenities of the civilized world."

A *tad* rough around the edges? A *tad*? That understatement was a record even for the British.

This was no boy. This was a motorcycle gang in battered jeans, bomber jacket and rough-out boots. A pirate with piercing blue eyes, stubble darkening his jaw and unruly black hair in need of a cut. She had expected him at the worst to resemble his twin brother, Dominic, who worked for her as a part-time accountant. But this man was nothing like harmless, middle-aged Dominic. There wasn't a bald spot or an ounce of fat anywhere on this guy. And he was anything but harmless.

Surely there was a mistake.

Another equally disturbing concern struck. If this was Daniel, and she prayed he wasn't, could John have sent him to spy on her, suspicious that *she* was responsible for the money missing from the restaurant accounts?

Fighting panic and forcing a bland expression she didn't feel, Stephanie took a small step back. The stranger was too close, too threatening.

"Are you Daniel?"

One corner of his mouth quirked. "And if I say no?"

If he said no? What kind of introduction was that?

She blinked several times, then drew upon a glib tongue and a sharp mind to gloss over her real feelings. "Then I'll assume you're the plumber, at which rate you're five days late and fired."

He laughed, a quick flash of white teeth in a sun-burnished face. *Oh, my.*

"To save myself that indignity, I'll confess. I'm Daniel Stephens, your new flatmate."

She'd always enjoyed the British male voice with its soft burr in the back of the throat. But this man's voice was half purr, half gravel and all male, a sound that shimmied down her spine to the toes of her new heels.

Heaven help her. What had she agreed to? This could never work. Not even if she wanted it to. And she most decidedly did not. He was too rugged to be handsome and too blatantly male not to be noticed. And Stephanie did not notice men. Not anymore.

She couldn't meet his gaze but she couldn't take her eyes off him either.

Her silence must have gone on a bit too long because he said, "May I come in?"

Stephanie opened the door wider, determined to remain as composed as possible under the circumstance. "Of course. Please."

She couldn't let him know how much his size and strength and sheer manliness unnerved her. She could handle him. Hadn't she determined long ago that no man would ever get close enough to hurt her again? Hadn't she rid herself of that fear by moving far, far away from Colorado?

"I'm afraid you caught me by surprise." A lie, of course. "The flat is…"

He poked his rather unkempt, and altogether too attractive head inside and finished her sentence. "Fine."

Her flat, like her person, was always ultra-clean and tidy. Outward appearances were everything. And having things out of place distressed her.

Stephanie turned and led the way to the living room. Her stomach jittered and her heart raced, but she was good at the pretense game.

Trouble was, it had been a while since she'd had to pretend quite this much. Or for quite this long. There was that troubling question again. How long would he be here?

Daniel's bulk filled up the large living room as if it were elevator-small. He glanced around with an unconcerned expression. The luxury of a flat that most could only dream of was apparently lost on him.

"Where should I stash my bedroll?" He swung the

bag from his wide shoulder as if it contained nothing but packing peanuts. "Any place will do. A room, the floor, the couch. Makes no difference to me."

Well, it certainly made a difference to Stephanie.

"I've put you in the back guest room." She forced a smile. "I assure you, it's more comfortable than the floor."

And as far away from her room as possible.

She led the way down the short hall toward the back of the flat, pointing out the other rooms along the way.

"This is the kitchen here. You're welcome to make use of it anytime." She felt like a Realtor.

"I wouldn't think you'd need much of a kitchen with the restaurant below."

"A person tires quickly of too much rich food."

"I can't imagine."

She paused to look at him. Bad decision. "Are you making fun of me?"

"Am I?" Blue eyes glittered back at her, insolent eyes that challenged. Stephanie glanced away.

Perhaps her statement had been rude. The man *had* spent a lot of years in places where food such as that served in the Bella Lucia was unheard of.

He was the boss's son. She didn't want to get off on the wrong foot with him. "I apologize. I'm really not a snob. But you'll have to understand, I'm accustomed to living on my own." She pushed the door open to the last bedroom. "You have your own bathroom through here."

"Nice," he said, though his tone indicated indifference as he gazed from the sage and toast décor to the queen-sized bed and then to the pristine bathroom beyond. He tossed the duffel bag into a corner next to a white occasional table. "I can see you aren't nearly as happy to have me here as John thought you'd be."

Stephanie wasn't certain what to say to that. She loved her job and couldn't chance upsetting her generous employer.

"I'm sure we'll get on fine." She hovered in the doorway, eager to have him settled, but equally eager to make her escape.

"I don't think you're sure of that at all."

He moved across the room in her direction. Stephanie resisted the urge to shrink back into the hallway.

"I don't know what you mean."

"Sure you do."

Before she knew what he was about, he touched her forearm. The gesture was harmless, meaning only to convey reassurance. It had just the opposite effect.

Try as she might to stand her ground, Stephanie flinched and pulled away, desperate to rub away the feel of his calloused fingers against her flesh.

Hand in mid-air, Daniel studied her, clearly bewildered by her overreaction.

"I meant no harm, Stephanie. You're quite safe with me here."

Right. As safe as a rabbit in a fox's den.

Forcing a false little laugh, she tried to make light of her jitters. "I'm sure all serial murderers say the same thing."

"Cereal murderers?" He dropped his hand and slouched against the door facing, too close for comfort. "Can't imagine harming an innocent box of cornflakes."

So, he had a sense of humor. She backed one step

out into the hallway. "My oatmeal will be relieved to hear that."

"Ah, now, porridge. There's nothing innocent about horse feed cooked to the gooey consistency of wallpaper paste. I might be tempted to do in a few boxes of those, after all."

This time Stephanie laughed. For a barbarian, he displayed a pleasant sense of the ridiculous.

"There's tea in the kitchen if you'd like a cup." She started back down the hall.

"Sounds great. If you're having one too."

She hesitated in the living-room entry, not wanting to appear rude, but certainly not wanting to become friends. Her idea of a male friend was one that lived somewhere else. Preferably Mars.

The gravelly purr moved up behind her, too close again. "We might as well get acquainted, Stephanie. We're going to be living together."

She wasn't overly fond of that term, but it wouldn't do to offend the son of her employer. From the rumors astir in the restaurant, she knew Daniel and Dominic were John's only sons, the result of a fling he'd had as a young man. Though he'd only recently discovered their existence, Mr Valentine was trying hard to make up for lost time.

"All right, then. I have a few minutes." She really should go, get away from him while she could still carry on a lucid conversation. Trouble was he'd be here when she came back.

In the kitchen, she poured tea into two china cups and set them on the small breakfast bar.

Daniel, instead of taking a seat, made himself at home by rummaging about for milk and sugar. In the narrow kitchen, they bumped once. Stephanie shifted away, rounding the bar to sit opposite him. If Daniel noticed her avoidance, he didn't react.

Instead, he slouched into the straight-backed white chair and splashed a generous amount of milk into the cup. Stephanie had never embraced the English penchant for milk in her tea. She did, however, favor sugar. In abundance.

"Tsk. Tsk. Three sugars?" Daniel murmured when she'd doused her cup. "Bad girl."

An unwanted female reaction skittered through her. The words were innocent enough, but his sexy tone gave them new meaning. Either that or she was losing touch with reality.

She inclined her head. "Now you know."

A black eyebrow kicked upward. "Sweet tooth?"

"A decidedly evil one. Grabs me in the middle of the night sometimes." Why was she telling him this?

"You don't look the part." His laser-blue gaze drifted over her slim body, hesitating a millisecond too long.

"I jog. I also have enormous self-control." Like now, when I really want you out of my flat, but I can't say so.

"Don't tell me you never sneak down to the restaurant for cheesecake and chocolate sauce?"

She smiled in spite of herself. "How did you guess?"

Small crinkles appeared around his eyes. The African sun had been kind to him. "Because that's what I'd do if I lived over a restaurant."

"Which you now do." Unfortunately.

"But you hold the keys to the Bella Lucia."

She stirred the spoon round and round in her cup. "There is that."

"Think I can persuade you to make your midnight runs with me in tow?"

Perhaps not, big boy.

Without comment, she lifted her cup and sipped.

Daniel did likewise, eyelids dropping in a soft sigh of appreciation. Stephanie had a hard time not staring. Though she was loath to admit it, Daniel Stephens was a stunningly attractive man.

"Can't get tea like this where I've been," he said, clattering the cup onto the saucer.

"Tell me about Africa." As she'd done countless times, Stephanie slipped into hostess mode, tucking away real feelings to skim the surface of civilized conversation. "Your father's very proud of what you've done there."

His face, so full of pleasure moments before, closed up tight. "My father doesn't know a thing about my work."

And from the stormy look of him, Stephanie figured John might never know. Her boss might want to mend fences with his sons, but this one had some hostility that might not be so easily overcome.

Daniel's anger reminded her of the kids she sometimes worked with in special art classes. There, where she volunteered her time teaching troubled children to paint, she had learned to listen as well as to share simple techniques of line and color.

In the same quiet voice she used to encourage those kids, she said, "Would you tell me about it?"

Forearms on the table edge, he linked his fingers and leaned forward. Too close again. The man had an unpleasant habit of invading her space. Stephanie tilted back a few inches.

"The work is rewarding and equally frustrating," he said.

So he'd chosen to sidestep the issue of his father and move on to the safer ground of Africa. She didn't know why she'd felt compelled to dig into his personal life in the first place. The less she knew about him, the better.

"Is that why you quit?"

"I didn't quit. I'll never quit," he said vehemently. "But I've finally realized that I can make more of a difference here than I can there."

She frowned, not following. "How?"

"To build sustainable, safe water systems takes money and expertise. I'm a civil engineer. I've spent my whole life dealing with the problem. I have the expertise. What I lack is that vulgar little commodity called money."

"So you're back in England to raise money, then."

"In a manner of speaking. I'm starting my own business, contracting water projects throughout England. The demand is high, especially in the area of flood control. A man who has the right skills and contacts can make a fortune."

Maybe he *was* as giving as John had indicated. "And you're planning to use that money to fund projects in Africa?"

"It's the best way I can think of." He shoved a hand over dark, unruly hair. "That's why I'm grateful to you for sharing this flat, and that's also why I agreed to the arrangement in the first place. I dislike accepting favors, particularly from my father, but the less spent on living expenses, the more I can spare for Ethiopia."

Despite her determination not to get too close, Stephanie's opinion of Daniel rose several notches. He had a caring heart, at least where the needy in Africa were concerned. This knowledge gave her hope that he would not be difficult to room with. If her luck held out, he would keep his distance until the business was started and he could afford his own place to live.

And this brought her to the question that had burned on her mind since that first telephone call from Mr Valentine. Just exactly how long would all that take? How long would she have this disturbing, intriguing, terrifying man living in her flat?

Because, for her own protection and peace of mind, the sooner he was gone, the better.

CHAPTER TWO

SURREPTITIOUSLY, Daniel watched the stunning red-haired woman from behind his teacup. The moment she'd opened the door he'd lost his breath, knocked out by the sheer beauty of her long legs, slim, shapely body, and the long, wavy just-got-out-of-bed hairstyle. Though her dress was mid-calf and modest, his first, very wayward thoughts had been of sex, a natural male reaction that he'd reined in right away. Mostly. He'd once had a penchant for redheads and, if his body's reaction was an accurate indicator, he still did. But he was here on business. And business it would remain.

A few minutes in her company, however, had told him what the old man hadn't. That she wasn't all that thrilled to have him here. But he was here and planned to stick around. And it didn't hurt at all that his flatmate was gorgeous and smelled incredible as well. He could look, but that was the end of it.

Long ago, he'd come to grips with his own short-comings where women were concerned. He liked them, enjoyed their company, but he'd never been able to fall in love. After too many years, he'd finally faced reality. Thanks to his mother, he lacked the capacity to love anybody.

"I need to get back down to the restaurant." Stephanie's teacup rattled against the saucer as she set it in place. "There's more tea if you want it."

"Thanks, but no. No time like the present to get started on the telephone contacts."

She reached for his cup and he handed it over.

"You should consider getting a mobile phone."

"Hmm. Possibly later." Right now he was conserving funds.

"I have a computer if you need one." She motioned toward the hall. "Sometimes I work on orders and supplies at night."

"I'll probably take you up on that." He pushed up from the chair and came around the bar to stand beside her at the sink. "Let me help with this."

Wariness flickered across her pretty face. "I have it."

"Okay." He backed off, wondering if his size intimidated her. She wouldn't be the first, though she reached his shoulders. He propped his backside against the blue granite counter several feet away from her. The tension eased.

With a grace that had him watching her hands, she washed the cups, dried them and placed them, handles aligned to the right, inside the cupboard. The orderliness of her flat was almost amusing. His idea of domestic order was keeping the mosquito net untangled around his face at night.

She tidied up, putting everything away until the kitchen looked as if no one lived there. In fact, the entire flat had that look. As if it were a photograph, a perfect, sophisticated, contemporary ad of an apartment. Not a lived-in place.

Folding a snowy tea-towel into a precise rectangle, she hung it neatly over a holder, straightening the edges while she spoke. "Is there anything else I can show you before I go? Anything you need?"

"I'm not a guest, Stephanie. No need for you to fret over me. I can find my way around." Hadn't he fended for himself as long as he could remember?

"Right. Of course." Her hands fidgeted with the edge of the towel. "I'd better go, then. The evening crowd begins soon."

"I may go out this afternoon myself. Do you have an extra key to the flat?"

She clasped the butterfly hands in front of her. "I'm sorry. I never thought of having another key made."

"Give me yours and I'll go to the locksmith."

"I'll get it." She looked none too excited about the prospect of sharing her key with him, but she disappeared down the hall and was back in moments, key extended. "This also fits the doors leading out onto the balcony. In case you didn't notice, there are two entrances to the flat. A staircase up the outside as well as the elevator in back of the restaurant."

"Good to know. Thanks." He pocketed the key, keeping watch on her fidgety movements. She'd relaxed somewhat since his arrival, but Daniel had the strongest feeling her tension was more than the normal discomfort of acquiring an unfamiliar flatmate. Though good breeding or schooling gave her the right words to say, her real feelings lay hidden behind the serenely composed expression. And yet, her hands gave her away.

With an inner shrug, he dismissed the idea. Stephanie's problems were her own. He wasn't interested in getting past the pretty face and tantalizingly long legs. His business here was exactly that—business.

"You're welcome to come down to the restaurant later and get acquainted if you'd like," she said, heading for the door. "Some of your family may come round. They often do."

The comment brought him up short. He still had trouble thinking of the Valentines as family.

"Is Dominic working today?" He'd had little time with his twin since returning to England. Discovering that Dominic had become a part-time employee of the restaurant below added to the appeal of living here. They'd been apart a very long time.

Stephanie glanced at her watch. "He should be in his office about now. I'm sure he'd enjoy a visit."

And so would Daniel, though he was every bit as eager to begin setting up appointments. The list of contacts in his bag was impressive. With it, his business should be up and running in no time.

His flatmate was halfway out the door when she stopped and turned. "Oh, one more thing, Daniel."

"Yes?"

Cool aqua eyes assessed him. "If you don't mind my asking, how long are you planning to be here?"

"Why, Stephanie—" he playfully placed a hand over his heart "—I'm crushed. Already trying to get rid of me?"

"No, no, of course not. I didn't mean that at all. I was just thinking…"

He knew exactly what she was thinking, but he couldn't accommodate her. "New businesses take a while to get off the ground. A year. Perhaps longer." He watched her, hoping to gauge her true reaction, but she gave nothing away. "That won't be a problem, will it?"

"That will be…fine," she said.

Daniel didn't believe a word of it.

Several hours later, Daniel exited the tube in high spirits, returning to Knightsbridge after a successful afternoon. He'd found a locksmith to cut a new flat key and afterwards had spent an hour chatting up a former university mate about business prospects. All in all, a good beginning.

Above ground, the rain had begun in earnest. Though he'd failed to bring an umbrella, the smell of rain in the air and the feel of it on his skin were a pleasure after years in the African sun. He resisted the childish urge to lift his face and catch the drops on his tongue.

At the back door of the Bella Lucia, he shook himself off to spare the floors a puddle. A kitten, no bigger than his hand, meowed up at him in protest.

"Sorry there, little one." He scooped the ball of fluff into one hand and slid her inside his jacket while he looked about for a dry place. She snuggled close, a warm, damp ball against his shirt, and turned her motor on. Daniel spotted an overhang and withdrew the kitten from his jacket. She meowed again.

"Hungry?" he asked, crouching down to set her

beneath the overhang. Her yellow eyes blinked at him. With a final stroke of the small head, he decided to steal a bite for her later, and then went inside the Bella Lucia to find his brother.

To the right of the wide entry were the lift and a door marked "Storage." On his left were the offices. Taking a guess, he tapped at the first one and went inside. Dominic sat at a desk, intently staring at a computer screen.

Daniel stood for a moment, observing his brother at work. Fraternal twins, they had once shared similarities, but now, beyond the blue eyes and tall stature, they bore little resemblance. Domestication and long hours in a high-pressure accounting firm had taken a toll on Dominic's once powerful physique.

"Careful there, brother. You'll be getting eye strain from all that hard work."

The balding head lifted with a smile and a brotherly jab. "No chance of that happening to you, now, is there, mate?"

"Not if I can avoid it," he joked in return. Hard work was all he'd ever known, as Dominic well knew.

A bit wearily, Dominic removed a pair of reading glasses and rubbed at his eyes. "Are you settled in, then? Finding the flat upstairs to your liking?"

Daniel flopped into a chair. "You know I don't care about the flat. Why didn't you warn me about my flat-mate?"

"Warn you?" Humor glinted on Dominic's tired face. "About what?"

"That she was young and beautiful. And not nearly as willing to have me move in as John let on."

A slow smile crept up Dominic's cheeks. "You always were a sucker for redheads."

"Getting this business off the ground is my first priority. The flat is just a step in that direction."

"Then why is Stephanie a problem? Did she try to toss you out?"

"No, nothing like that." Quite the opposite, actually. "She was polite, accommodating." She'd put on the pretense of welcome, but her fidgety movements told a different story.

"Then what's the problem?"

He wasn't sure how to answer that one. "I make her nervous."

Dominic guffawed. "Look in the mirror. You make everyone nervous."

Daniel shoved a hand through his unruly hair. He never could figure out why his appearance concerned people. Just because he didn't care about the usual conventions of dress or style, people sometimes shied away. Or maybe it was the darkness. Dark skin, dark hair. Bad attitude.

But this wasn't the feeling he had with Stephanie. "I think the problem is deeper than the way I look."

"Shave. Get a haircut. See if that helps."

He'd skip that advice. Unlike his conservative, by-the-book twin, Daniel had never been a suit-and-tie kind of a man. Perhaps that was why he meshed with Africa so well. That, and the fact that Africa needed and appreciated him.

"Is there a boyfriend lurking around to punch my face for moving in with her?"

"I thought you weren't interested."

"I'm not dead either."

Dominic chuckled. "Good. You were starting to worry me."

"I gave up on love, not on life."

Dominic knew better than anyone about Daniel's empty heart.

"Sometimes they're one and the same."

The profound statement stirred the old restless longing, the feeling that, no matter how much good he did, life was passing by without him.

"Are you going to annoy me about my nonexistent love-life or tell me about Stephanie Ellison?"

"Well, let's see." Dominic gnawed at the earpiece of his glasses, pretending to think. "She doesn't allow staff to smoke anywhere near the restaurant. Says it projects a bad image to the customers."

"That's not exactly the kind of information I meant."

"None of us know much about her before she came here. She's a mystery really."

A mystery. Hmm. Better steer clear of that. He had enough puzzles to solve with the new business. "What kind of manager is she? Demanding? Difficult to work for?"

Though Dominic had only been in this job just over a week, he was good at gathering information, a knack that also made him a good accountant. Most of the time he knew more about a company than the owner.

"Stephanie's a bit of a workaholic, a real control freak about tidiness," Dominic said, "but she treats employees well. She gives every appearance of being an excellent manager."

Daniel heard the subtle hesitation. "What do you mean by 'gives every appearance'?"

"Nothing really. She's doing a fine job." Dominic glanced away, fidgeted with his glasses. He was holding back.

"I know you, Dominic. What are you not saying?"

"I don't want to spread unsubstantiated rumors."

"I'm your brother. I've just moved in with the woman. If she's trouble, you have to tell me."

"All right, then, between you and me." He sighed and rolled a squeaky chair back from the desk. "You've heard about the money missing from the restaurant accounts?"

Daniel nodded, frowning. John had mentioned the problem. "You think Stephanie's involved?"

"No. I don't. Someone kind enough to take sick waiting staff to her flat, give them an aspirin and take over their shift while they rest isn't a likely thief. Plus, she's meticulous to the point of obsession about every detail of running this place. I can't see her dipping into the till."

"Yet, someone is responsible."

"Right. And she's the newcomer, the outsider."

"Not the only one," Daniel pointed out.

Dominic blinked, clearly shocked at the suggestion. "You think I—"

Daniel laughed. "Not in a million years." His straight-down-the-line brother was so honest, he'd often confessed to childhood mischief before being confronted. "Have you talked to John about it?"

"Actually, the first clue came from him. He asked me to balance the dates when the money disappeared with all the other transactions filtering in and out of the three restaurants. There were some interesting inconsistencies, but nothing definite yet."

"So what's your decision? Is our pretty manager guilty?"

"I'm still watching, but, like I said, I don't want to think Stephanie is involved. She isn't the type."

Daniel didn't think so either, though he barely knew the woman. He'd much rather believe her anxiety around him was personal than an embezzler's guilty conscience.

The idea gave him pause and, before he could stop the words, he asked, "What about her personal life? Does she see anyone?"

Dominic tossed his glasses onto the desk and tilted back, his gaze assessing. Daniel shifted in his chair. Okay, he'd admit it. He wanted to know about his flatmate as a woman, not as a restaurant manager.

"She goes out now and then, though the gossip mill says she never dates seriously."

"Why? Too busy with work?"

"That's my guess. But Rachel thinks she's had her heart broken."

"Rachel?" Daniel frowned. "Employee or relative?" He was having trouble keeping track.

"A cousin. Our uncle Robert's daughter. Her sister, Rebecca, is a close friend of Stephanie's. I think she may know more about your lovely manager than anyone."

"She's not *my* anything," Daniel groused. "I was just asking." And he didn't know why, so he decided to let the subject of his flatmate drop. "So, tell me about you, Dominic. How's the job? The family?"

Dominic's gaze flicked to the computer screen. He picked up a pen and twirled it in his fingers.

"Alice is pregnant again."

Daniel tried not to let the surprise show. Dominic looked stressed enough without being reminded that his other kids were nearly grown. "How many does this make? Four? Five?"

Daniel spent so little time in England that he couldn't keep up. Never fond of his brother's wife, he hadn't tried too hard. Alice's well-to-do family had vigorously protested when she had married a nobody like Dominic, and since then she had maintained an air of superiority that rankled Daniel.

"This makes four." Dominic ran a hand over his face, and Daniel noticed again how much his brother had aged. "Alice is thrilled. She thinks another baby will keep us young. And a new addition also gives her a reason to shop."

As if she needed one. Daniel remembered his sister-in-law's propensity for spending. Luckily, his brother had done so well that his family could afford the best of everything. They lived in a fashionable area of London. His children attended private school, and both Dominic and Alice drove a Mercedes. Holidays in Rome or Madrid or anywhere they fancied were the norm. Daniel was glad for his brother's success.

Dominic had only taken the extra position here at the restaurant as a way to get acquainted with the family he'd never known, and now to help ferret out the thief in the ranks. He certainly didn't need the money.

"What about you? How do you feel about a new baby?"

Dominic drew in a deep breath and let it slowly out. "Stunned. I never expected to be a father again at forty."

"Forty's not too old."

"Easy for you to say," Dominic said with a rueful grin. "You aren't losing your hair."

Daniel returned the grin. "Is Alice all right, then? The pregnancy going well?"

"Sure. Everything's fine. Great. You'll have to come to the house for dinner one night and see for yourself." He gave a self-conscious laugh. "Get that haircut first, though."

In other words, Alice would have a fit if her uncivilized brother-in-law embarrassed her in front of her friends.

"How about one night next week?" Dominic went on. "I'll invite John as well."

"I don't think so."

"Come on, Daniel. Don't be a hard case. We wanted a father all our lives and now we have one. He wants to get to know us."

Tension coiled in Daniel's gut. John Valentine was not his favorite subject. "He has a daughter—he adopted Louise; he wanted her. Why would he want to know us?"

"Because we're blood. You and I have a right to be in this family."

"Not according to Ivy." John's wife had thrown a fit to discover her husband had two sons with a former lover. "And maybe she has a point. Being adopted is better than being illegitimate." The word left a nasty taste in his mouth.

"Louise doesn't think so. She's very upset. She's

even started one of those birth-parent searches. Has John worried sick. He says she's not herself at all."

"Do you blame her? This must be a terrible shock to her." It had been to him. And he blamed the parents, not the children. Though he'd only briefly met Louise, she seemed nice enough, a quiet, accommodating woman dedicated to her family. She didn't deserve to be blindsided by two long-lost brothers and the revelation that she had been adopted by John and Ivy Valentine.

"Maybe." Dominic lifted a doubting brow. "Maybe not."

"Meaning?"

"John phoned earlier, fretting over her as usual. Which is very bad for his heart, by the way, and she well knows that. Says Louise is planning to leave for Meridia tomorrow for some nonsense. A make-over, I think he called it, for Emma."

Daniel searched his memory banks but came up empty, sighing in resignation. "Am I supposed to know Emma?"

"Cousin. Yet another of Uncle Robert's numerous offspring. Emma's the chef. Quite a renowned one, I hear. She was commissioned for a king's coronation. That's why she's in Meridia though who knows why Louise thinks she needs a make-over."

"Ah." Not that Daniel comprehended any of this. After living a lifetime with a handful of family to his name, he was now swimming in relatives he didn't know. From Dominic, he knew that their father John and his half-brother Robert were at odds. He also knew that the recent death of their grandfather William had increased the rivalry and battle for control of the restaurants. Beyond that, Daniel was lost. Even if he cared, which he hadn't yet decided if he did or not, sorting out all the Valentines would require time and exposure. "So how does this relate to our sister?"

"Our father thinks Louise is going off the deep end and needs him more than ever." His nostrils flared. "I think she's an attention seeker, drumming up sympathy to keep a wedge between John and his blood children."

"You and me."

"Right. She's on the defensive, trying to hold John's allegiance. After growing up in the wealth and society that actually belonged to us, she's unwilling to share. I, for one, think it's time you and I reaped the benefits she's had all her life."

The answer bothered Daniel. Though he didn't necessarily feel the same, he could understand his brother's emotional need to embrace their birth family. But he and Alice were well set. They didn't need the Valentine "benefits", either social or financial.

Settling back against the plush office chair, he studied his twin. They had always been different, but in the years since they'd spent any real time together the differences had increased tenfold.

Daniel wasn't sure he liked the changes.

CHAPTER THREE

FEET propped on a chair, Daniel slouched in broody silence on the too-small red sofa. His belly growled, but the half-eaten fish and chips on the table had long ago grown cold and greasy. Papers, phone numbers, business cards and other evidence of a budding business venture lay strewn around him in the darkness. He should be satisfied. But he wasn't.

Except for a few, brief conversations Stephanie Ellison had avoided being alone with him since his arrival. She was friendly enough when he went into the restaurant. She even smiled indulgently at his feeble jokes and brought him a drink. But long after the restaurant closed, she remained downstairs.

And he wanted to know why. This was her flat. She should be comfortable here even with him present. Worst of all, he didn't enjoy feeling like an interloper. He'd had enough of that when he was a kid and Mum brought friends to their hotel.

So tonight he'd waited up for little Miss Manager.

When her key turned in the lock and she walked in, Daniel was ready for her.

Light flooded the room.

"Are you avoiding me?"

Stephanie looked up, manicured fingers on the light switch, clearly startled to find him still awake, sitting in the midnight darkness. "I beg your pardon?"

"You heard me."

She didn't answer. Instead, she took one glance at the flat and started her incessant tidying up.

"Leave it," he growled, annoyed that once again she was trying to sidestep him.

She kept working. "My goodness, you're in a mood tonight. What's wrong?"

"You." Actually, she wasn't the only problem, but the one he wanted fixed first. The others could wait.

Her fidgety hands stilled on the fish and chips wrapper. "And just what have I done that's so terrible?"

"You skip out of here at pre-dawn, seldom come up to your own flat throughout the day, and then sneak in long after I've gone to bed."

"Managing a restaurant requires long hours." She tossed his forgotten dinner into the bin and then turned on him, green eyes flashing. "And I do not sneak."

"Have you always worked eighteen-hour days? Or only since taking me on as a flatmate?"

She gathered the papers from the floor and made a perfect stack on the table. "Why are you asking me this?"

"Just answer the question. Are you avoiding me?"

"Of course not. How ridiculous."

"Good. Then stop clearing up my mess and come sit down."

"I've worked all day and I'm very tired."

"You *are* avoiding me. All I'm asking is a few minutes of your time. We are flatmates, after all. We live together, but one of us is not living here." Daniel didn't care that he sounded like a nagging wife. He wanted to know what her problem was.

She rolled her eyes. "Okay. Fine. I'll sit."

And she did. Like a gorgeous red-plumed bird, she perched on the edge of a chair opposite him ready to fly away at any moment. Her hands twisted restlessly in her lap. He had the strongest urge to reach over and take hold of them.

"I haven't ax-murdered you in your sleep, have I?"

Her lips twitched. "Evidently not."

At last. He was getting somewhere, though why he cared, he couldn't say.

"So stop being so jumpy." It irritated him.

"I am not—" But she didn't bother to finish the denial. "What do you want to talk about? Is there a problem with the flat? A problem with the new business?"

"Do you ever relax? Maybe read a book or watch the telly?"

"When I have time."

Which he doubted was ever.

He pushed. "How much of London have you seen since you've been here?"

"Not nearly as much as I'd like, but I love it. The museums, the history."

"We're steps away from some of the finest museums in the world. Which ones have you seen?"

"The Royal College of Art," she shot back.

No surprise there. He knew from looking at the walls

in the flat and in the restaurant that she fancied modern art, the kind he couldn't begin to understand. There wasn't a realistic picture anywhere in the place.

"Where else?"

She shrugged and went silent.

"That's it? You've not done the palace or the Victoria and Albert Museum?" They were right around the corner.

"Not yet. But I will."

"What about Hyde Park?"

"I jog there."

"A picnic is better. What say we have one?"

Her hands stopped fidgeting. "A picnic?"

Was that longing he heard?

"Yep. Tomorrow afternoon. Hyde Park."

She shook her head; waves of red swung around her shoulders. "I'm too busy."

"So am I." Suddenly, he wanted a picnic more than anything. "But real life happens in between the busyness, Stephanie."

Her gaze slid up to his, slid away, then came back again. She wanted to. He was certain of it.

He gave her a half smile. It probably looked sinister but he hoped for charm. "Avoiding me again?"

"No!"

He lifted a doubting brow.

She sighed. "All right, then, a picnic. Tomorrow after the noon rush."

Triumph, way out of proportion to the event, expanded in Daniel's chest. At last. He was getting somewhere with the cool and aloof one. Though why it mattered, he had no idea.

* * *

"You're going on a picnic?" Chef Karl, slim and neat in his burgundy chef's coat, froze with one hand on the parmesan and the other on a giant pan of fresh veal.

"Yes, Karl, a picnic," Stephanie said coolly, though her nerves twitched like a cat's tail. "Not bungee jumping from the London Bridge."

"But—" his wide brow, reddened by heat and concentration, puckered "—you never take time off."

"She is today." Daniel, purring like an oversized pussycat and resembling a pillaging pirate, burst through the metal swinging doors that led into the kitchen from the back of the restaurant.

Stephanie's twitchy nerves went haywire. She had to grab on to the stainless-steel counter to, literally, get a grip.

My goodness, that man takes up a lot of space.

Karl, who hadn't a subtle bone in his body, looked from Stephanie to Daniel. "Oh. I see."

Exactly what he saw, Stephanie didn't know and didn't want to know. The staff had no right to poke into her personal life, although she now realized she and Daniel would become this afternoon's gossip.

Great. She was already struggling with last night's decision. What had she been thinking to agree to such a silly thing? Such a dangerous thing? But the truth was she wanted to go on a picnic. With her new roommate. And she did not want to obsess over the reasons.

When she'd come in last night to find Daniel sitting in the dark surrounded by his usual mess, she'd been tempted to run back down the stairs. He was right. She *had* been avoiding the flat, partly because of him. Partly because she dreaded the nightmares that had begun with his arrival.

She was exhausted both physically and mentally. When he'd goaded her, she'd been too tired to think. And now, here she was, both dreading and longing for a picnic with a pirate.

"Don't worry about it, Karl." She patted the chef's arm. "I'll prepare the lunch myself. This is a restaurant, you know. We're bound to have something picnic-worthy around here. You go ahead with preparations for this evening."

"Anything I can do to help?" Daniel asked, eyes dancing with a devilish gleam that said he didn't give a rip about becoming the latest fodder for gossip.

"You could let me off the hook." But she hoped he wouldn't.

The gleam grew brighter. "Not a chance. Be ready in ten minutes. We're walking."

Then he shouldered his way out of the kitchen, slowing long enough to hold the door for one of the hostesses.

"Bossy man," Stephanie muttered half to herself.

"The macho ones always are," the blonde hostess said. "But they are *so* worth it."

Stifling a groan, Stephanie settled on simple picnic fare, which she packed into a bread basket before going out to check the restaurant one more time.

Only a few stray shoppers sipped lattes or fragrant teas at this hour of the day. The dining room was quiet except for the efficient staff preparing for later when things really got hopping. Everything was well-organized. Stephanie's sense of order was intact—

except for the little matter of an afternoon with a most disorderly man.

She passed by the bar, scanning the stock, the glasses, the bartenders. A lone customer sat at the bar sipping one of their special hand-mixed drinks. As was her habit, she stopped to offer a smile and a welcome.

From the corner of her eye she spotted Daniel's dark head. He poked around behind the bar and came out with a bottle of wine. He held it up, arching an eyebrow at her.

She pointed a finger in chastisement, but he only laughed and tapped a wide-strapped watch. "Two minutes. Back door."

As soon as he was out of hearing distance, Sophie, one of the bartenders, leaned toward her. "You and Delicious Dan seem to be hitting it off nicely."

Stephanie frosted her with a look. Grinning, Sophie slunk away to polish glasses.

Two minutes later, basket clenched in chilled fingers, Stephanie joined Daniel in the hallway. Her pulse, already racing, kicked up more when John Valentine walked in the door.

Her boss's portly face lit up. "Daniel. Stephanie. What a delight!"

Beside her, Daniel stiffened. "John."

They exchanged greetings, but Stephanie could feel the tension emanating from Daniel and the disappointment from her boss.

"So," John said, somewhat too jauntily. "Are the two of you off somewhere, then?"

"Hyde Park and the Serpentine. Stephanie hasn't

been." Daniel's response was almost a challenge, as if he expected argument.

Guilt suffused Stephanie. She shouldn't be running off to play with the boss's son. "I hope you don't mind, Mr Valentine."

"Mind? Why should I? You hardly ever take an afternoon."

Since his mild heart attack a few weeks back, Stephanie thought John looked tired. With all that was going on, she wondered how his health was holding up. Missing money was bad enough, but the family problems continued to mount. John's wife was still angry about the arrival of the twins, though John longed to get to know them. Then there was his daughter, Louise. She'd had a whirlwind trip to Meridia and then, instead of working through her problems with John, had already jetted off again. This time to Australia to meet a woman who could be her biological sister. And none of that included the lifelong bitterness between him and his brother, Robert. How much more could the poor man handle?

"Are you sure, Mr Valentine?" she asked. "I can stay here if you prefer." In fact, considering the way Daniel got under her skin, working would probably be wiser.

"I'm available if any problems arise in the dining room. Go on. Have a lovely time. I'm going to pop in and say hello to Dominic. He thinks he may have some news for me."

With a fatherly pat to Daniel's shoulder, he left them. Daniel stared at the closing door, expression wary and brooding.

"Are you all right?" Stephanie asked.

His jaw flexed. "Why wouldn't I be?"

Then he took the basket from Stephanie's hands, pushed the back door open, and led her out into the overcast day.

The walk to the park was much more pleasant than Stephanie had anticipated. After the encounter in the hallway, she'd expected dark silence. Instead Daniel provided a wickedly humorous and totally cynical commentary on élite London that had her laughing when they entered the beautiful park.

The laughter of children sailing toy boats along the Serpentine Lake wafted up to them from a hundred yards away. A cool breeze, in line with the glorious autumn day, played tag with the curls around Stephanie's face. Daniel's hair, too, rugged and unruly, was tossed by the wind. His was the kind of hair a woman wanted to touch, to smooth back from his high, intelligent brow, to run her fingers through.

The thoughts bothered her and she forced her attention to the wonders of the historic park, breathing in the scent of green grass and fall flowers. "This is a gorgeous park."

"You can thank Henry VIII. He acquired it from the monks."

"Acquired?"

The corners of his eyes crinkled. "In much the way he *acquired* everything."

"Ah, bad Henry."

"Not all bad. We're here, aren't we?"

Well, there was that.

They passed kite flyers, strolling mothers, moon-eyed lovers, and other picnickers before finding a clear shady area to spread their blanket.

Daniel did the honors, flapped the red and white cloth into the breeze and then collapsed on it as it settled to the grass.

"Here you go, m'lady," he teased. And with one jean-jacketed arm, he exaggerated a flourish. "The finest seat in all of London."

Legs carefully folded beneath her, Stephanie sat on the edge of the blanket as far from her companion as was polite. He puzzled her, did Daniel Stephens, vacillating from broody and cautious to light-hearted in a matter of minutes.

Stretched out upon his elbow like some big cat basking in the sun, he seemed happier in the outdoors, as though the inside of buildings couldn't quite contain all there was of him. His mouth fascinating in motion, Daniel chatted tour-guide style about Rotten Row, famous duels, kings and queens, regaling her with stories of the famous old park while she emptied the contents of her picnic basket.

"I suppose we could have got food here," he said motioning to the eating places sprinkled about.

"I wouldn't have come for that. Only a picnic."

"Woman, you crush my fragile ego. I thought you came for my charming company."

She snorted. To her delight, he fell back, clutching his chest. "And now you laugh at my broken heart."

Relaxed and enjoying herself more than she'd thought possible in the company of a barbarian, she thrust a sandwich toward him. "Here. Try this. Karl's tarragon chicken salad is guaranteed to cure broken hearts as well as crushed egos."

"Yes, the way to a man's heart and all that." He unwrapped the sandwich and took a man-sized bite. "Mmm. Not sheep's blood or lizard's eyes, but it will do."

"You haven't actually eaten that sort of thing?"

He arched a wicked brow. "When in Rome, do as the Romans. When in Africa…"

She lifted a bunch of fat grapes. "Suddenly, these don't look too tasty."

"Very similar to lizard's eyes. Right down to the squish."

She made a stop-sign with her palm. "Hush."

Unrepentant but thankfully silent, he reached for the grapes. With an air of mischief he studied one closely, then met Stephanie's gaze before popping it into his mouth.

Refusing to watch, Stephanie said, "If we have time later, I'd like to walk awhile."

"We'll make the time." He tossed a grape into her lap. "A long walk after a picnic is good for the soul."

She could certainly use that.

"I wouldn't know. I've never been on one." She tossed the grape back to him. It thudded against his chest.

"You've never been on a walk?" Head back, Daniel threw a grape high into the air and caught it in his mouth.

Stephanie tried to look away and failed. "No, silly. A picnic."

Another grape had winged upward. Daniel let it plop onto the blanket uncaught.

"Never? No childhood jaunts to the country? No egg sandwiches in the garden?"

"No. My family was far too stuffy for that. Little girls sat at the dinner table, learned to play hostess, and never, ever got dirty."

"Unbelievable."

"Yes." And I don't want to talk about it. Some things didn't merit conversation at a girl's first picnic. "You, on the other hand, look perfectly comfortable sprawled beneath a spreading chestnut tree with a sandwich and a bunch of grapes."

"Far more my style than your fancy London flat."

"Is that why you're so messy?"

He tapped her shoe. "I'm not messy. You're far too tidy."

"That's been said about me before. I'm just a perfectionist."

"What makes you so obsessive about it?"

She wasn't going down that road either.

"There's nothing wrong with order," she replied, more defensively than she'd intended.

"Never said there was." He levered up to rummage in the basket, coming out with the wine and two glasses swiped from the restaurant. Following another foray into the basket, he extracted a corkscrew. With little effort on his part, the cork slid out with a pop.

Daniel widened his eyes at her. Stephanie giggled. She didn't know why, but a popping cork always made her laugh.

He poured, handed her a glass and waited while she sipped.

"You have good taste in wine," she said, savoring the rich flavor on her tongue.

"I have good *luck* in wine. Don't know a thing about the stuff."

"Really? I thought a son of John Valentine—"

"I wasn't always John's son. Remember? My mum was a club singer. Not the worst, but not the best either. Our upbringing wasn't quite on par with the Valentines." He made the admission easily, but some of his conversational ease had seeped away.

"Did you grow up here in London?"

"All around England. Wherever Mum could get a gig."

"That must have been an interesting life."

"Not really. Hotel staff make good nannies for a day or two but they don't substitute well for parents." Bitterness laced his words, telling Stephanie she'd touched a nerve. His meaning was clear. Two boys left alone to fend for themselves in strange hotels could not be the best situation.

"I'm sorry you were unhappy." And she was. Very sorry.

He shifted his attention from her to a red-dragon kite floating overhead. "Being alone all the time is scary to a little kid. And confusing."

Stephanie's heart squeezed. It couldn't have been easy for him to tell her such a thing, but the peek into his unhappy childhood made him seem less intimidating, more approachable. And she liked him for it.

"What about when you were older?"

"Then we were terrors." The mischief was back. "Pounding on guests' doors at two o'clock in the morning.

Dumping ice over the balconies onto unsuspecting passers-by. We got our mum kicked out of more than one fine establishment."

Stephanie chuckled. "I can see you doing that. You bad boy."

He toasted her with his glass and knocked it back in one drink. "All Dom's idea, I assure you."

"It was not." She couldn't imagine easygoing Dominic coming up with any mischief on his own. If ever there was a by-the-book, rule-following man, it was Dominic Stephens.

"You're right. I was the rabble rouser." He sighed, a happy sound, and flopped onto his back. "Poor Dom."

She smiled down at him, trying to imagine him as a child. He was so completely man. But he'd been a little boy once, and he'd been wounded in the process.

Something in that knowledge caused her to relax. She had nothing to fear from Daniel. He knew about heartbreak too.

Daniel reached up and wrapped his fingers around a lock of her hair. He tugged, pulling her down toward the blanket. Slowly, she gave in to the gentle pressure and reclined on the soft flannel, the wineglass discarded in the grass.

He didn't touch her, for which she was grateful. She wasn't ready for that yet.

The thought caught her by surprise. *Yet?* She would never be ready for that. Daniel might have an alluring charisma about him, but so had Brett. Worse yet, so had Randolph.

She shivered and pulled her sweater closer.

Though Daniel didn't move or speak, she felt him there, warm and appealing. After a few seconds, she gave in to the quiet and closed her eyes, relaxed by the wine.

The breeze whispered against her face. In the distance a victory shout went up as one boater bested another. In her imagination, she could hear the clip-clop of royal carriages and envision the elegantly clad ladies from times gone by.

Something tickled her nose. She wiggled it. The tickle came again. She pushed at it and received a purring chuckle for her efforts.

Lazily, slowly, she opened her eyes to see Daniel hovering above her, a blade of grass between thumb and forefinger. Before she could stop the instinctive reaction, she cringed.

He pulled back. "Hey. I didn't mean to startle you."

Her heart hammered crazily. "I must have dozed."

He continued to hover, muscled forearms holding him above her. His eyes darkened in concern. "You're shaking."

She managed a false laugh. "It's nothing. A sudden wake-up."

Daniel brushed a hair from the corner of her lips. He let his fingers linger on her cheek, his gaze searching.

Stephanie froze, breath lodged in her throat. She didn't want him to remove his hand, though common sense said to do so. She lay there, examining the emotions as the therapists had taught her, until she knew—*she knew*—she wasn't afraid of Daniel. At least, not for the usual reasons. If she had fear, it was of herself, because she couldn't start a relationship with this man. She couldn't go there again and face the inevitable rejection. Years of counseling had brought her this far, but she'd long ago decided being alone was easier than risking heartache.

And Daniel could easily be a danger to her fragile heart.

"Let's walk," she said, her voice a breathy murmur.

Though obviously full of curiosity, Daniel helped her to her feet without comment. Shakily, she gathered the remains of their picnic, looking around for a garbage can. She'd hardly touched her chicken salad. No wonder the wine had rushed to her head.

They fell in step, strolling toward the long bridge spanning the lake. Daniel didn't try to take her hand and she was grateful. She knew he wanted to, but he must have known she would pull away.

In silence now, they walked over the bridge, pausing at the top to lean on the rails and look down. On the shore two lovers lay stretched upon the grass. The young man kissed his girlfriend with such tenderness that Stephanie's chest ached. She glanced away. But the view of a young family, doting over an infant in a stroller, was no better.

Today seemed to be the day to stir her latent domestic urges. Perhaps it was the amazing and romantic news that Emma, one of the Valentines and head chef at the Chelsea restaurant, had married a king. Or worse, maybe Daniel was to blame.

She slid a glance in his direction. The brooding Daniel had returned, staring in dark silence at the kissing lovers.

Being with him turned her thoughts in strange directions, down roads she'd closed long ago.

Unintentionally, she sighed. Daniel's dark head slowly swiveled in her direction. She kept her focus trained on the happy little family below.

Once, a long time ago, she'd believed she could break free from the past and embrace the future with a loving husband. She'd even dreamed of having a child to cherish. But Randolph had made sure that could never happen. That no man would ever want her.

Yes. Long ago, she'd come to grips with her inevitable destiny. So why did the thought depress her so much today?

CHAPTER FOUR

IN THE days to follow, Daniel had a hard time getting that picnic out of his mind. Correction. He had a hard time concentrating on business instead of his copper-haired flatmate. He had discovered that he was not only attracted to Stephanie, he also liked her. She was witty, and when she let her guard down, she was warm. It was that guard that puzzled and challenged him, and he reckoned the challenge was the fascination. That was why he couldn't get her out of his mind.

He loved challenges. Why else would he try to single-handedly solve the water-shortage problems of African countries?

He watched her flit around the living area, doing her usual fussy tidying-up thing. The television blabbed in the background and lemon furniture polish fragranced the air.

Daniel was supposed to be working at the desk he'd set up in one end of the large reception room, but he watched her instead.

Tonight, she'd come up from the restaurant early, claiming the flat needed cleaning. Yeah, right. The only mess was his and he couldn't bring himself to feel bad over it.

She'd changed into casual trousers and top and pulled her hair into a loose, sexy knot on top of her head. Wispy tendrils played around her elegant cheekbones, tempting him.

He shifted restlessly and tossed down the pen. He'd been celibate too long.

Last night, he'd heard her in the throes of a nightmare. He'd wanted to go to her but had resisted. What help could he offer? That sort of involvement required emotion, and he didn't have that in him. Besides, he doubtless would not be welcome in Stephanie's bedroom, bad dream or not.

He pushed up from the desk and stretched to relieve the kink in his back. When he turned, Stephanie knelt on the floor, polishing an end table. She looked up, luscious mouth curved in a smile. Daniel experienced another of his wayward, unflatmate-like thoughts.

"You've been working hard," she said. "Any progress?"

"Actually, more than I expected. My father—" he could barely say the word with civility "—has offered his support."

"Daniel, that's awesome." Her eyes glowed with true pleasure. "He has contacts that can give your business a real boost."

Daniel didn't answer. How did he admit that he didn't trust the man who had given him life?

Stephanie stopped polishing to study him. "You don't exactly seem overjoyed."

"I don't understand why he wants to do this."

"Because you're his son."

"He doesn't even know me. He has no idea if I can do the work, or if I have the integrity to carry out these projects in an ethical manner."

"That's right." She aimed the cloth at him. "Yet, he's willing to introduce you to some influential people. He's willing to put his name and reputation on the line."

"Yeah." And Daniel didn't get it. What did the old man expect in return? What was his game? Nobody did something for nothing. "He's set up a lunch meeting with some important investors over at the other restaurant."

"Are you going?"

"I haven't decided." He didn't like favors. They obligated.

Folding the polishing cloth into her usual crisp rectangle, Stephanie stood and faced him. "You didn't ask my advice, but I'm giving it anyway. Go. From all I've observed in a year of working for the man, John's a good guy."

Yeah? Then where was he when I was a kid?

"I'll think about it." He turned his attention to the television, hoping for distraction. All this talk about his father annoyed him. "Let's watch a movie."

She put away the cleaning materials and surprised him by coming into the living room instead of scuttling off to hide in her bedroom. Perhaps he could thank the picnic for this new acceptance of him. Though she'd fallen into some kind of mood at one point, they'd had a great time.

He still couldn't imagine that a woman her age had never experienced a picnic. Must have come from a weird family. He pointed the remote and clicked. Who was he kidding? His hippie mother had been super-weird. They'd gone on lots of picnics, though hers had usually been Woodstock-style outings that had lasted days during which he and Dominic had wandered around on their own.

He flipped through the channels, stopping at a comedy program.

"How's this?"

"Anything's okay with me. A brainless way to relax."

"You actually do that on occasion?" he asked.

She made a face at him. The curled nose and squinted eyes looked cute. The long legs curled under her looked pretty interesting too. Who knew naked toes could stir a man's libido?

Better concentrate on the comedy instead. He did, but his attention kept straying back to his companion each time she laughed.

Eventually, the program finished and the barrage of advertisements began. When he was about to give up and go back to his desk, a news brief flashed across the screen. A beautiful little girl, no more than six, smiled from a photo while the reporter intoned a gruesome story of neglect and abuse and violent death.

Stephanie slapped both hands against her ears and squeezed her eyes closed. Daniel was tempted to do likewise.

"Horrid, isn't it?" he asked, stomach roiling.

"Dreadful." She pushed off the couch and turned away from the television, her complexion gone pale, tears glistening in her eyes. "That poor little angel."

He knew she had a heart for troubled kids and

sometimes taught an art class for some kind of scheme. Naturally, she'd be disturbed. Who wouldn't be?

"Yeah." He scrubbed a hand over his face, repulsed at the inhumanity of some people. If a hard-heart like him was troubled, tender-hearted Stephanie would make herself sick if she dwelled on the story.

He switched the telly off. The room went dark except for the dim hall light. Quiet, broken only by the traffic on the road below, enveloped them.

"Would you like some tea?" he asked, feeling the inexplicable need to comfort her.

She shook her head. "I need to run downstairs."

Her comment felt odd somehow. He squinted at her, tall and slim and composed, and wondered if he'd missed something. "At this hour?"

"One of the dishwashers was acting up earlier, had a small leak. I want to check it."

Daniel frowned at her. Why hadn't she mentioned this earlier?

"I could have a look. I'm handy with water pipes and such."

"No need. Really. I'll handle it."

In other words, she didn't want his company, a truth that caused an unwanted curl of disappointment.

"All right, then. Ring me if there's a problem."

Without answering, she headed out the door.

Daniel jumped into the shower for a quick scrub and had just stepped out when the telephone rang. He grabbed for the receiver.

Stephanie's breathy voice said, "Daniel, come quick. I need you badly."

He didn't hold back the chuckle. "Well, that's more like it."

"I'm serious. Please, if you think you can help, come down here."

A surge of renewed energy zipped through him. "The dishwasher?"

"Leaking everywhere. I'm slopping up water now."

"Will you feed me cheesecake afterwards?" referring to the time he'd asked her to take him down for a midnight snack and she'd frozen him with silence.

"What?"

"Never mind. Be right down."

Stephanie squeezed out yet another mop full of water and watched in dismay as more seeped from beneath the industrial-sized dishwasher. She'd called the plumber again about this a week ago and still he had yet to show up. Ordinarily, she'd have followed up and called someone else, but she'd had too many other problems on her mind. One, the money missing from the accounts.

Two, Daniel Stephens. Since the moment he'd arrived, the man had occupied her thoughts in the most uncomfortable way. Then he'd taken her on that picnic and she'd realized why. She liked him. His passion for Africa stirred her. His relentless pursuit of an incredibly lofty goal stirred her. Looking at him stirred her.

A voice that also stirred her broke through the sound of sloshing water. "Ahoy, mate. Permission to come aboard."

Stephanie looked up. All she could think was, *Ohmygosh. Ohmygosh.*

She'd known he was coming. She'd been expecting him. But she hadn't been expecting this.

Barefoot and shirtless, Daniel waded toward her in a pair of low-slung jeans, a tool belt slung even lower on his trim hips.

Close your mouth, Stephanie. Mop, don't stare.

But she stared anyway.

Daniel Stephens, dark as sin, chest and shoulder muscles rippling, black hair still wet and carelessly slicked back from a pirate's forehead, was almost enough to make her forget the reasons why she could not be interested in him. Almost.

Slim hips rolling, he sloshed through the quarter inch of water to the dishwasher. Dark hairs sprinkled his bare toes.

The sight made her shiver. When had she ever paid any attention to a man's toes?

"You forgot your shirt," she blurted, repeating the slogan seen everywhere in American restaurants. "No shirt, no shoes, no service."

He grinned at her, unrepentant. "You said you needed me. *Badly.* How could I not respond immediately to that kind of plea from a beautiful woman?"

He thought she was beautiful? The idea stunned her. Beautiful? Something inside her shriveled. How little he knew about the real her.

He, on the other hand, was hot. And he knew it.

"Are you going to fix that thing or annoy me?"

One corner of his mouth twitched. "Both, I imagine."

He hunkered down in front of the washer, tool belt dragging the waist of his jeans lower. Stephanie tried not to look.

"Do you think it's bad?"

"Probably have to shut down the restaurant for a week."

Stephanie dropped the mop. It clattered to the floor. "You've got to be kidding!"

He twisted around on those sexy bare toes and said, "I am. It's probably a leaky hose."

"Can you fix it?"

He smirked. "Of course."

"Then I really am going to fire that plumber."

"Go ahead and sack the useless lout. Tell him you have an engineer around to do your midnight bidding."

Now, *that* was an intriguing thought.

She retrieved the mop. "Which is more expensive? A plumber or an engineer?"

White teeth flashed. "Depends on what you use for payment."

Time to shut up, Stephanie, before you get in too deep. Do not respond to that tempting innuendo.

Metal scraped against tile as he easily manhandled the large machine, walking it away from the cabinet to look inside and behind. Stephanie went back to swabbing the decks. Watching Daniel, all muscled and half naked, was too dangerous. Thinking about that cryptic payment remark was even more so.

"Could you lend a hand over here?" he asked.

Oh, dear.

The floor, dangerously slick but no longer at flood

stage, proved to be an adventure. But she slip-slid her way across to where Daniel bent over, peering into the back of the machine.

"What can I do?"

"See this space?"

Seeing required Stephanie to move so close to Daniel that his warm, soap-scented and very nude skin brushed against her. Thankful for long sleeves, she swallowed hard and tried to focus on the space in question.

"Down there where that black thing is?" she asked.

"Your hands are small enough, I think, to loosen that screw. Do you see it?"

"I think so." She leaned farther into the machine, almost lying across the top. Daniel's warm purr directed her, too close to her ear, but necessary to get the job done.

"That's it. Good girl."

His praise pleased her, silly as that seemed.

He pressed in closer, trying to reach the now-unfastened hose. His breath puffed deliciously against the side of her neck. Stephanie shivered and gave up trying to ignore the sensation.

Their fingers touched, deep inside the machine. Both of them stilled.

Her pulse escalating to staccato, Stephanie's blood hummed. As if someone else controlled her actions, she turned her head and came face-to-face with searing blue eyes that surely saw to her deepest secrets.

She needed to move, to get out of this situation and put space between them. But she was trapped between the machine, the hose, and Daniel's inviting, compelling body.

"I think I have it," she said, uselessly. Foolishly.

Daniel's nostrils flared. "Yes. You certainly do."

His lips spoke so close to hers that she almost felt kissed.

Daniel held her gaze for another long, pulsing moment in which Stephanie began to yearn for the touch of his lips against hers. How would they feel?

All right, she told herself. That's enough. Stop right now before you venture too close to the fire and get burned.

With the inner strength that had kept her going when life had been unspeakable, she withdrew her hand and stepped away.

As though the air between them hadn't throbbed like jungle drums, Daniel didn't bother to look up. He finished repairing the hose while Stephanie completed the mopping-up and tried to analyze the situation. Daniel was interested in her. Big deal. In her business, she got hit on all the time.

But it wasn't Daniel's interest that bothered her so much. It was her own. Something in Daniel drew her, called to her like a Siren's song. One moment he was cynical and tough. The next he was giving and gentle. There was a strength in him, too, that said he could—and would—move a mountain if one was in his way. He was different from anyone she'd ever met.

Metal squealed against tile again as Daniel shoved the washer back into place.

"All done." He gathered tools, dropping them into the proper slots in his belt. "You'll need to order in a new hose right away, but that should hold for now."

"Thank you. I really appreciate this."

He came toward her, all cat-like muscle and unquestionable male. "How much?"

"What do you mean, how much?" She took a step back.

He took one forward. "Remember your promise?"

Mind racing, she held the mop out like a skinny shield. What had she promised?

He stopped. "Cheesecake?"

"That's it? Cheesecake?"

"Why, Stephanie, whatever were you thinking?"

She laughed and playfully shoved the mop at him. He ducked, one hand out to ward off the pretend blow.

And then the slick floor took control. Daniel's bare feet slipped. Tools rattled and swayed, throwing him more off balance. He reeled backwards, caught the counter with one hand but not before his head slammed against the jutting corner.

Stephanie dropped the mop and rushed to his side. "Daniel. Oh, my goodness! Are you hurt?"

He righted himself, rubbing at the back of his head. He felt ridiculous. One minute, he was about to kiss a beautiful woman. The next he was thrashing around like a landed salmon.

"Only my pride," he admitted.

But when he brought his hand forward from the aching lump on the back of his head, blood covered his fingers. "Uh-oh."

"Let me see." Stephanie tugged at his shoulders. "Bend down here, you big lug."

With a half-grin, half-grimace, he lowered his head. A minute ago she'd been backing away as if afraid he'd touch her. And now her hands were all over him in gentle concern. Puzzling, infuriating woman.

"A scratch, I think. It's nothing." But her cool fingers felt good against his skin.

"Let me decide that." All business, she guided him to a chair. "Sit. We keep a first-aid kit beside the stove."

"I'm all right. It's only throbbing a bit."

But he sat anyway while Stephanie got the kit and went to work cleaning up the wound.

As soon as her fingers touched his hair, he forgot all about the throbbing pain. When had a woman last touched him with such gentleness?

The throb in his head moved to his heart.

"How bad is it, Doc?" he managed, though her touch was causing more reaction inside his head than outside.

"Irreparable brain damage. I fear there's no hope."

He hid a smile. If this was what it took to get her to touch him and joke with him, he'd bash his head every day of the week.

"Can't you kiss it and make it all better?" A man could always hope.

Her fingers stilled, only a fractional second, but enough for Daniel to know the question got to her. Good. She was thinking about it, too. He'd thought of little else tonight. Well, other than cheesecake. He still had hope in that department.

"Kissing spreads germs," she said lightly. "Can't chance infection."

"I'm already hopelessly damaged. A few extra germs won't hurt." He twisted around. "What if I said please?"

Their eyes met and, for once, held. Yes, she was

thinking about it every bit as much as he was. What he couldn't work out was why he didn't just go ahead and kiss her. He wasn't shy with women. He didn't feel shy with Stephanie. But she kept a barrier up at all times, a wall that held him back, that scared him a little, as if kissing her would open a Pandora's box he was unprepared to handle.

Stephanie broke the stand-off by bopping him playfully on the shoulder. "Behave yourself or I'll use this alcohol cleanser."

"Evil woman." But he leaned his head forward so she could examine the cut.

Her stomach brushed against his bare back as she gently separated layers of hair to dab away blood. Her scent, as clean and elegant as the woman herself, wrapped around him. Her fingers, light, deft, flitted over his scalp with exquisite care, as if she feared hurting him.

Daniel closed his eyes, soaking in the sensation. His own mother had never touched him with such infinite tenderness, and the truth of it brought a lump to his throat. A yearning, far greater and more complicated than desire, expanded his ribcage with a hot ache.

He wanted her never to stop, and that worried him. He, who'd made a point never to need anyone ever again, needed something from Stephanie.

He slept in the same house with her, breathed in her perfume, wondered what she wore to bed. But while he knew her on the surface, he sensed a secret heartache hidden behind the serene face. He needed to know what had hurt her. And that worried him even more.

"This would be easier if you had less hair."

Instantly, Daniel roused out of the pleasant lethargy that enshrouded him.

"Are you saying I need a haircut?"

He hadn't expected her to be like his sister-in-law, so concerned about appearances. But then, of course she was. Didn't her magazine-perfect flat prove as much?

"Maybe a trim."

She was probably right. He rubbed at the whiskers around his mouth. Lately, they'd taken the shape of a Fu Manchu. "What about this?"

"Your stubble? I like it."

Once again, he twisted around, this time surprised and far too pleased. "You do?"

"Sit still." She pressed gauze against the back of his head and held tight. "Yes, I like it. Very much. It's…" Her voice trailed off as if she had already said too much.

"Sexy?"

"Roguish." She gave his shoulder a soft pat. "There. All done."

Daniel caught her wrist. "Roguish?" Slowly, he pulled her around the chair to stand in front of him.

"Daniel—" She lifted a finger in warning.

He was tempted to bite it. "I only want to say thank you."

"Workman's compensation," she teased. "You were wounded on the job."

She started to pull away but he held fast. Her playfulness became a flicker of worry. Puzzled, he released her. He didn't want her to be anxious. He wanted her to be… What *did* he want?

She didn't move, and he was even more puzzled.

He studied her, trying to gauge what was going on inside her head, wondering why she fascinated him so much.

He wanted to reach out and bring her closer, but, more than that, he wanted her to come to him. He wasn't even sure where this was going, but, for purely selfish reasons, he longed for her to make the first move.

Something was churning behind that pretty face and he was willing to wait her out.

In that split second when he thought she might relent and move closer, a commotion erupted outside the restaurant.

CHAPTER FIVE

STEPHANIE jerked as if she'd been shot.

"What on earth—?"

Daniel leaped to his feet, grabbed a pipe wrench from the counter, and stormed through the swinging doors toward the back of the restaurant.

"Be careful, Daniel." Seeing no other weapon, Stephanie yanked a copper pot from the overhead rack and followed closely behind, too jittery to remain in the kitchen without him. After all, the hour was late, they were alone, and someone *had* been stealing money from the restaurants.

"Stay back," Daniel cautioned, putting one hand behind him in the dark hall to stop her.

"No," she whispered fiercely, bumping up against those wide, strong fingers.

Her own hands trembled on the pot handle, though she wasn't certain if they trembled from fear of the noise or from the unsettling episode with Daniel. She couldn't stop thinking of the feel of his hair, the soapy scent of his skin, or his bereft expression when she'd started to pull away.

Yes, something in him called to her, a loneliness she understood and wanted to erase.

"Stay behind me, then," he murmured. And the command made her feel protected in a way she'd seldom experienced. No one ever protected her except herself. And many times she'd done a sorry job of it.

At the back exit, they paused to listen. The racket had subsided. Slowly, Daniel eased the door open. In one swift motion he flipped on the light and leaped outside, wrench at the ready.

Then he laughed.

"Daniel?" Stephanie lowered the pot.

"Come out here."

She did. Two garbage cans lay on their sides, spilling trash on the concrete. A tiny kitten tore at a discarded meat wrapper.

Stephanie gazed at the pot in her hand and the wrench in Daniel's. "Look at us. Aren't we brave?"

"Positively formidable."

"Two giants bearing weapons against this terrifying intruder."

They both looked at the little kitten and burst into laughter.

In the crisp autumn darkness, with a soft breeze carrying scents of exhaust and the promise of winter hovering above, Stephanie and Daniel stood in the alleyway and laughed like lunatics left too long beneath the moon.

The kitten took note of their presence and, with a plaintive cry that resembled recognition, abandoned the trash heap to weave zigzags through Daniel's legs.

"Daniel," Stephanie said, pretending scandal. "Have you been feeding this cat?"

"Apparently not enough." And they laughed some more, letting the tensions and questions brewing between them be washed away in the ridiculous.

"Come on," she said when she could once more breathe. "Let's feed your protégé."

"What about me? I'm still craving that payment you offered. Engineers don't work for free, you know."

Stephanie figured the moon had stolen her sanity. "Cheesecake?"

"Unless you have something else in mind." He grinned wickedly. "Terms are negotiable."

Her stomach fluttered. She really should send him upstairs for a shirt, but, at this point, what did it matter?

They scavenged the kitchen, found some smoked salmon for the kitten and two large pieces of cheesecake and a jar of chocolate sauce for themselves.

Rather than turn on the lights of the dining room and alarm security patrol, Stephanie lit a candle. Encased in a ruby globe, the candle glowed red and fragrant on the small table next to the kitchen door.

"Good cheesecake." Daniel laid down his fork. "But I need more chocolate."

She handed him the jar. "Karl is an excellent chef, especially with the desserts. They tell me your cousin Emma is every bit as good. Too bad Bella Lucia has lost her."

"She's the one that married the king, right?"

"Yes. In Meridia. Wherever that is."

Daniel poured the sauce on his plate, watching the chocolate drip with a mesmerized expression. "If I were the King of Meridia, there's no way my new wife would be commuting to a job in England. She'd definitely stay at home."

"Hey, don't hog all that." She playfully grabbed the jar from him. "So you're going to make someone a very bossy husband?"

"I'll never know the answer to that." He caught a final drip of gooey sauce on his finger and licked it. "Daniel's rule number two. Never waste good chocolate."

She added another dollop to her plate. "What's rule number one?" she asked, expecting him to elaborate on his marriage comment.

"Empty your boots before putting them on." When she laughed, he said, "I learned that one the hard way. Scorpions." He gave a fake shiver.

"Africa must be an astounding place."

"You'd love it, Stephanie. The different countries, all the colors and sounds and smells. And the people I met. Amazing. Especially in the small villages. They may only have a small bowl of food for the entire family, but they'll insist on sharing with a stranger."

Everything about him changed when he spoke of Africa. The cynicism slipped away. His face lit up with an energy that came from loving what he did.

"How did you end up working so far from home?"

"Adventure. A chance to get away from a troubled upbringing." He hitched a bare shoulder, an action that flexed the muscles of his chest. "All the usual reasons of reckless youth."

"Interesting that your twin didn't join you."

"Dom and I have always been different." He licked

the back of his fork and then studied it. "He's even more different these days, though. More intense, stressed."

She could hear the concern in his voice and admired him for that. Never having had a sibling, she couldn't imagine the bond twins might have. "I assumed that was his personality, him being an accountant and all."

"Didn't used to be. Oh, he's always been a stickler, always following the rules."

"Unlike you?" Stephanie teased.

"Exactly. That's why he's a great accountant and I'm not." Daniel's mischievous eyes twinkled. "But in the past, he was looser, more relaxed, a real joker at times." He shook his head and made another stab at his cheesecake. "He has a lot on his mind, I guess. A baby on the way, teenagers."

"That's trouble enough right there. But the restaurant has also added to his workload. That could be part of the problem. John has him auditing all the accounts in search of the money that's gone missing." She leaned her elbows on the table and admitted, "Did you know I thought you were a spy?"

His fork clattered to the table. He touched his chest, an eyebrow arched in question. "A spy? Like 007?"

Stephanie laughed. "Not quite, but I wondered if John thought I had something to do with the missing money."

"You do have access."

His words stunned her. Did he think she was responsible? "I don't need money, Daniel. And I love my job. I would never do anything to jeopardize these restaurants."

He held up a hand to stop her defense. “I know that now, Stephanie. I didn’t when I first came here.”

“So you *were* a spy? John set this little arrangement up as a means to keep an eye on me?” The notion mortified her.

“Not even close. In fact, it’s a silly idea. John and I aren’t on what you would call intimate terms.”

“Am I a suspect?” Her stomach hurt just thinking such a thing.

“The subject came up, but Dominic doesn’t believe you’re involved, and he says John feels the same.”

Some of her tension ebbed away in the gentle reassurance. She respected her boss. To think he might suspect her hurt. But she appreciated Daniel’s honesty in telling her. “You had me scared for a minute. I thought the Valentine clan had turned on me.”

“I don’t consider myself a Valentine, Stephanie. John hasn’t discussed any of this with me at all. I’m not part of the inner circle.”

She could see that bothered him. “You really should try to get to know them. Especially your father and your sister.”

A shadow, caused by more than the candle, fell across his handsome face.

“Adopted sister,” he said firmly.

“And pretty upset to learn that, from what I hear. She’s always been the darling in that family, Daniel. The sweet, good child doted on by all. To suddenly discover she’s adopted must have totally rattled her foundation, her sense of self.”

“I can relate to that,” Daniel said. “But I can’t understand why John and Ivy kept the adoption secret in the first place. Now they have to deal with the unpleasant consequences."

Glad to leave the unsettling subject of the missing funds, she said, "You mean the trip to Australia to find her biological sister?"

He nodded. "That's great from my viewpoint, but John's ranting that he doesn't want her poking into the past. Thinks she should be content with the life he gave her. Rather selfish of him, don't you think?"

Stephanie shook her head. "I think he's afraid she'll get hurt. That these biological relatives won't be what she expects or that they'll somehow take advantage of her."

His mouth curled cynically. "He's more likely worried about how this will affect him and his business. He doesn't need Louise creating more difficulties for him."

"So bitter, Daniel. John's made mistakes. Who hasn't? But he cares for Louise. You and Dominic, too, if you'll give him a chance."

Daniel twirled circles in the chocolate sauce on his plate. "Why bother? He seems to make a habit of hurting his children. Louise had a right to know she was adopted, just as Dominic and I had a right to know who our father was."

"Agreed. But that's the past. There is nothing you can do about it now." She was a fine one to be talking. "But you *can* affect the future."

"My future is set." But his tone was defensive, uncertain.

"Is it? Don't you want family, Daniel? Don't you

need people around you? People who care for you and will be there for you when life sends a crushing blow?"

He grew quiet, thoughtful, and she knew, for all his arguments to the contrary, Daniel needed to connect with his family. Like her, he was held back by the fear of getting hurt. Strange how knowing that made her feel closer to him.

Who was she kidding? She felt closer to Daniel than she'd felt to anyone in a long time. They were kindred spirits, both having childhood hurts that still hampered them as adults. A bond like that was a powerful thing.

"Change of subject, okay?" he said gently, tapping her fingernail with one tine of his fork. "My strange life doesn't concern you."

Oh, but it did. More and more every day.

The dark restaurant, the ruby candle glow, created an ambience of intimacy and, inevitably, personal conversation began to flow, moving away from the hazard of discussing his estranged family. He told her more about his gypsy lifestyle growing up. Stephanie sensed the hurt and loneliness interspersed with the funny stories.

In turn, she told him bits and pieces of her life in Colorado, her work in Aspen before coming here. But some things didn't warrant discussion, even with Daniel.

Long after the cheesecake was gone and the saucers pushed aside, they talked on. Stephanie knew the hour must be terribly late, but she didn't want to move, didn't want to leave this cocoon that had spun around them in the darkened restaurant.

Daniel leaned corded forearms on the table, his folded hands inches from hers.

"Tell me about the art classes."

"They're great. The kids—" She shrugged. "I like to think I'm helping, but I don't know." Some of them had been through far more than she had. "I want so badly to make a difference. Sometimes I dream about them, about their situations, about the things that have happened to them."

"You're doing a good thing, Stephanie. A good thing." He touched the back of her hand. "How did you get involved in that to begin with?"

"I've always had a heart for people who were down and out. I guess it stems from—"

She'd gone too far this time, letting the intimate setting and fatigue affect her usual reserve.

"Stems from what?"

Playing the pretense game didn't work too well with a bright man like Daniel. And in truth, she wanted to tell him. She was just too afraid, so she took the easiest way out.

"There was a child once, a little girl. A victim of abuse." The inner trembling started up, but Stephanie didn't let the nerves stop her. She could tell Daniel this much. And maybe by doing so, some of the lingering shadows would be driven back. "I should have told someone. But I didn't."

His voice deepened, incredibly gentle. "Why not?"

She lifted a shoulder. "She was afraid telling would make the problem worse. I didn't know what to do." And she still didn't.

Sometimes that was the worst shame. Knowing she might have stopped it, but she'd been too young to understand that.

As if he read her thoughts, Daniel asked softly, "How old were you?"

"Nine." She shook her head, recognizing the denial in his eyes. "But I should have told someone."

"You were a child. You can't feel responsible."

"I know. But it bothers me." Ate at her, if she told the truth. Had turned her into a woman who couldn't let anyone close enough to see the real person inside. "Children are powerless, Daniel."

He reached out, covered her hand with his. She soaked in the comfort of his spontaneous gesture.

"You were a child, too, sweetheart, as powerless as that little girl."

"I know. That's why I want to make a difference now. To help these kids, to show them a better way, a way out. I can't change the past, but I can help now."

The warmth of his skin against hers, his quiet understanding seeped into her battered heart like fresh rain into the cracked, parched earth. And like that dry ground, Stephanie felt renewed, refreshed, almost whole again.

For a split second, a blink in time, Stephanie considered telling him the rest, but as courage formed the words Daniel spoke again. "Life's injustices drive me crazy."

"Me, too. Obviously."

"Why is it, do you suppose, that some people have everything going for them and others have nothing?"

With relief, Stephanie recognized that she'd raised no suspicions. Daniel saw the conversation on the surface, as two adults discussing a troubled world.

"You're doing all you can to make a difference, Daniel, just like I am. In fact, more than I am. You've spent your whole life trying to help. That has to mean something."

"But the need is so vast, sometimes I feel like I'm trying to empty the ocean with a spoon."

Tenderness gripped her. "You have such a good heart."

"Stephanie, my love, let me tell you a fact about your flatmate. He doesn't have a heart." He said the words lightly, easily as though teasing, but she knew he was serious. "I'm a civil engineer. Developing water projects is what I do."

Stephanie didn't accept his reasoning. Pure self-interest would have lined his pockets long ago.

"What about feeding that kitten? Or coming down here in the middle of the night to fix my dishwasher? Is that for selfish reasons, too?"

"No. That's cheesecake."

The silly answer made them both chuckle.

"You ate that entire jar of chocolate," she said, smoothly, glad to move away from topics that could only lead to trouble.

Daniel took the empty container and scraped the inside with a spoon. "Wasn't I worth it?"

"Absolutely." She stole the jar from him and ran her finger around the edge.

Daniel grabbed her finger and licked it. The energy from the touch of his tongue against her skin raced through her body faster than a breath. For a guy without a heart, he had a habit of doing strange things to hers.

She pulled her hand into her lap, but the feel of that warm, moist tongue wouldn't go away.

"Don't try to steal my chocolate, buster."

Was her voice really that breathless?

"All's fair in love and chocolate."

"Now there's a subject we haven't discussed." She blamed the dark, intimate atmosphere for her bravado. But why not talk about love? They'd discussed everything else.

"Love?" Daniel shook his head. His hair, now dry and in need of a comb, flopped forward. "I'd rather have chocolate, thank you."

Her heart began to beat a little faster. "Haven't you ever been in love?"

"Thought I was once, but it didn't work out. Since then. Well, a man realizes his shortcomings. What about you? Any boyfriends wanting to bounce my head against the concrete?"

His airy tone gave her the courage to answer honestly. "I suppose I've realized my shortcomings as well."

"I beg to differ. No shortcomings from my perspective."

Though his observation did wonders for her self-esteem, it showed once again how little he knew of the real Stephanie.

"I was in love once, but…" Her voice trailed off. Why had she admitted that?

"And he hurt you."

The sentence was a statement, not a question, and Stephanie accepted that he understood what she'd left unsaid.

"Yes. In the worst possible way." Brett had rejected the real Stephanie, unable to see beyond the scars.

Compassion flared in Daniel's flame-blue eyes. She thought he might touch her. And she realized just how much she yearned for that. He, like no one else, found a way past her guard and into her heart.

"What did he do? Cheat on you?"

"No. Not that." Stephanie wished she hadn't brought up the subject, but didn't know how to stop now without drawing suspicion. They were tiptoeing far too near her secret shame.

Daniel's fingers flexed against the tabletop, his expression fierce and dangerous. "Don't tell me he hit you."

Stephanie tried not to react too strongly. She should have known he'd follow that line of thought. He was too smart not to make the leap of logic from cheating to abuse. She had to end it now.

"Let's don't go there, okay? This is not something I like to talk about."

He studied her in the dim candlelight for several heartbeats while her pulse thumped in warning. Finally, his rich voice quiet, he said, "All right. I'll let it go for now. But a woman like you shouldn't give up on love just because some fool didn't have sense enough to recognize a treasure."

"I thought you didn't believe in love."

"For myself, Stephanie. Only for myself."

Was he warning her off? Telling her not to feel anything for him? Not to fall for the gentle and kind man beneath the pirate's tough exterior?

If he was, she had a very bad feeling that his warning came too late.

From somewhere on the dark streets of London a clock chimed the hour. "Oh, for goodness' sake, Daniel. It's two o'clock."

She hopped up and began clearing away their dishes.

Daniel followed her into the kitchen where he stretched like a waking lion. “Doesn’t feel a moment after one to me.”

“We’ll both be terrors tomorrow on so little sleep.” She dumped the dishes in the sink and turned toward him. “Let’s go. These will wait.”

Daniel pretended shock and disbelief. “You’re leaving the dishes undone?”

Stephanie raised a defiant chin. “Yes, I am.”

“Will wonders never cease?” he said mildly. A smile quivered at the corners of his mouth.

As they left the kitchen, heading to the elevator, Daniel reached out, palm upward in invitation.

The night had been revealing and wonderful. And she’d begun to feel things she didn’t want to feel again. Things that could get her hurt. Only she worried that this time, with this man, the hurt would be too much to bear.

She slipped her hand into his, accepting the fact that, regardless of what the future held, Daniel Stephens might be worth the risk.

CHAPTER SIX

"SCISSORS. Scissors. My kingdom for a scissors."

Daniel rummaged through the kitchen drawers, came up empty and decided to breach the inner sanctum of Stephanie's bathroom. Surely the woman owned a pair of scissors.

Without a second thought, he charged into her bedroom and came to a sudden halt. Though he had passed by and glimpsed the sleek blue and gray interior, he'd never come inside this room. The essence of Stephanie filled the space.

The bed was fluffy, white, and feminine. A dressing table against a wide window that looked out over the city contained the usual pots and jars that he couldn't comprehend. The curtains were open; light flooded the room.

He drew in a lungful of Stephanie-scented air. That gentle, expensive scent had driven him quite mad last night in the restaurant. He could stand here all day breathing it in.

Above a white painted chest of drawers, a single painting compelled him to a closer look. In startling contrast with the elegant, oriental-influenced artwork in the rest of the flat, slashing colors tore at the canvas in a violent assault. Perfectly centered within the storm of blues and violet was a shattered heart. On each broken piece was a tiny tormented face, dripping blood and tears.

Puzzled over why Stephanie would choose such a disturbing print for her bedroom, he squinted at the name scrawled in one corner.

His mouth fell open in surprise. "S. Ellison."

He'd known she painted, but this turbulent look inside the artist was startling to say the least. As if beneath the aloof exterior lay an unreachable depth of emotion screaming to be released.

Intuitively, he knew she would not be pleased by his observation. Backing away, he went into the bathroom, once more to be assaulted by her scent. Perfume. Shampoo. Soap.

"Scissors, Daniel. Scissors." Annoyed, maybe even unnerved that Stephanie occupied so much of his thinking, he found the scissors and got out of her private space. The hall bathroom was safer.

"Where to start…" he murmured, peering intently into the mirror. He lifted one long section of hair and snipped. Not so good. But it was too late to turn back now.

A few chops and curses later, he heard the front door open and close.

"Daniel."

He poked his head around the doorway. "In the hall bathroom."

Stephanie's heels tapped against the tile.

"I just wanted to tell you—" She paused in the open doorway. "Oh, dear."

Their eyes met in the mirror. "That bad, is it?"

Her mouth twitched. He gave her his fiercest glare, which only made things worse. The twitch became a full-blown smile.

She took the scissors from his hand, an action that ensured he looked every bit as bad as he feared.

"Come in the kitchen and sit down."

"Why?"

She laughed. The woman actually had the audacity to laugh. "I'm going to save you."

"Can you?" he asked hopefully, feeling like an utter idiot, but relieved to know she could, and would, help out.

"I think so." She pulled a chair out. "Sit."

"Didn't we do this last night?" He squinted one eye up at her while she wrapped a towel around his neck and secured it.

"You seem to be having problems lately with your head."

"Tell me about it." She had no idea just how bad the problems *inside* his head were becoming. He looked doubtfully at the towel. "Does this have to be pink?"

"I will never tell a soul that the great Daniel Stephens, conqueror of Africa, marauding kittens and leaky dishwashers, wore a pink towel." She slid a comb through his hair, taking extra care over the cut from last night. "May I ask what brought this on?"

Hadn't she said he needed a trim? Not that he'd ever cared about appearances, but some people did. "Need to spruce up for that lunch meeting with my father."

She dipped around him, pleased. "You've decided to go?"

Thanks to her influence, but he didn't mention that.

"Good business sense, don't you think? Those men own companies that could easily fund a water system for an entire village."

"Good sense, indeed." She combed his hair toward his face. It fell over his eyes. "How much of this do you want off?"

"My fate is in your hands."

She giggled. "Oh, Daniel. Pink towel and all, you do live dangerously."

Curiously happy, Daniel settled back into the chair and closed his eyes. Having Stephanie's hands on him, however he could get them there, was worth the humiliation of a botched haircut.

He let that thought linger for a while, studied on it. She was good for him as well as good to him. Being with her settled some of the restlessness. Maybe even some of the anger.

Last night had been a turning point of sorts when she'd let him come close, and he'd exulted in the knowledge that she'd trusted him, at least a little.

Though she'd stopped short of telling him all he wanted to know about her former lover, Daniel wasn't obtuse. The man had hurt her badly, maybe even physically abused her, though he hoped he'd misinterpreted that part. The idea of a man hitting her sickened him, but it explained why she'd been jumpy and wary in the beginning. Trust wouldn't come easy after that.

Stupid as it was, he'd been glad for that leaky dishwasher. Was even tempted to tear up some of the other pipes so he could fix them for her and watch her face light up with gratitude and admiration. Sharing secrets and cheesecake with Stephanie was worth the lump on his head.

"You have wonderful hair." Her voice had grown quiet.

He tried to think of a witty comeback but failed. How could he when her slim, sweet-scented body kept inadvertently bumping his as she moved around the chair, snipping and combing?

He'd had plenty of haircuts in his life, but none like this. None with a woman who interested him so much, whose touch warmed a cold place inside him. He tried to shake off the feeling. He didn't do emotional commitments and, from what Stephanie had told him last night, he sensed her reluctance in that area as well.

He couldn't understand why the idea of commitment even occurred to him. He enjoyed women. Always had. So what was the big deal with this particular one?

A lock of hair tumbled down, tickling. Stephanie brushed it away, then unfastened the towel and whipped it off.

He opened his eyes.

The tingling in his scalp moved lower.

She was bent at the waist sweeping a mountain of black hair into a dustpan. He silently cursed the calf-length dresses she always wore.

"There you go. All presentable…" Her voice trailed off. Must be the dopey expression on his face. She slowly put the dustpan aside.

At the moment, Daniel didn't care if he had hair or not. He did care that Stephanie was standing in front of him looking incredibly kissable.

He wrapped his fingers around her wrist. The bone felt fragile, delicate within his work-strengthened grip.

"We started something last night that we never finished," he said. "I'm a man who leaves nothing undone."

"Daniel," she warned without much conviction.

Stormy green eyes held his and he saw a yearning there as strong as the one in his own heart. He waited until she made the decision to come to him and then guided her onto his lap.

He wanted this moment to last. Wanted to watch her face and eyes. Wanted to see the desire flame up in her. He'd seen the painting. He knew she was a woman who hid deep passion behind this perfect, cool demeanor.

She touched his cheek. Fingers of silk stroked from cheekbone to the corner of his mouth and rested there. And then she smiled. Tremulous. Uncertain.

Uncertainty?

An ache of exquisite tenderness squeezed the breath from him. No, it couldn't be tenderness. He didn't *do* tenderness. Must be desire.

And to prove as much, he kissed her.

She was more than he bargained for.

Her mouth was far sweeter, far hotter, and far more willing than he'd imagined. She kissed him back with so much passion, his head reeled. His pulse thundered like rampaging elephants, and a swirl of some frightfully unfamiliar emotion pushed inside his chest. *Sweet, sweet, sweet* was all he could think.

And then as quickly as the kiss had begun, it ended. Stephanie yanked back from him, her mouth rosy and moist and horrified. Her eyes, wide and stormy as the

Indian Ocean, darted frantically around the kitchen as if she had no idea where she was. She was shaking, though he didn't think from passion.

She leaped from his lap and rushed out of the room. Her bedroom door clicked shut with a little too much force.

He blinked at the empty kitchen. "What was that all about?"

With a vengeance, he kicked aside the chair and followed.

"Stephanie." He rattled the doorknob. Locked. "Let me in."

"Give me a minute." Her voice was shaky, strangled.

Oh, boy.

"Look. I'm sorry." Only that he'd upset her, not that they'd finally kissed. He shoved a hand over the top of his head, startled to have considerably less hair. "Will you tell me why you're upset?"

"I'm not upset."

An obvious lie. He blew out a breath.

"If you're worried about what people will think if we get, um, involved. I mean, because we're sharing a flat..."

"I'm not worried."

He gripped the back of his now hairless neck. "Okay, then. Good. I'm not, either."

When she didn't answer, he pecked at the door. "Steph. Listen. Remember what you told me last night, about the idiot that broke your heart?"

"Yes." Was that a smile in her voice? Maybe he was getting somewhere.

"No need to worry. The last thing I would ever want is to get involved. Emotionally, I mean. We both know up front that we aren't interested in that sort of thing. So we're safe. Right?"

With an abruptness that had him backing up to the far wall, the door opened and Stephanie came breezing out, every hair in place, lipstick refreshed, and no hint that anything had occurred. A warm, impassioned woman had gone into that room. The elegantly untouchable restaurant manager came out.

"Everything's fine, Daniel. Sorry for the overreaction to a little meaningless kiss." Tiptoeing, she kissed him on the cheek and then tip-tapped down the hall. "Gotta run."

A little meaningless kiss? Meaningless?

Daniel blinked at the slender backside disappearing around the corner.

He had never been so confused in his entire life.

Stephanie still shook as she entered the empty elevator. She hoped she looked more composed than she was feeling at the moment. Daniel had rocked her world. Completely. One kiss and she was lost for ever. Dear heaven above. She'd wanted the kiss to go on for ever, to always have Daniel's strong arms hold her as if he could shield her from the whole world. She'd felt so secure, so protected.

"I'm falling in love with him." Her throat tightened around the muttered words.

She'd suspected as much last night when they'd teased and talked in the restaurant. When the real man behind the pirate's face had revealed his true colors. Oh, she'd suspected her feelings for a while, but today had clinched it.

That was why she'd been so anxious not to let him ever touch her, kiss her. Deep down she'd known he had the ability to break down all her barriers and make her vulnerable again. Vulnerable, the one thing on earth she could never afford to be.

Daniel didn't want any part of love. Had even told her as much. She should be glad of that, considering her past. He probably wanted an affair. She didn't. Not that she didn't want him. But an affair meant revelation, and she couldn't allow him to discover the real Stephanie and be repulsed, as Brett had been. Besides, in the light of her deepening emotions, an affair that led to nowhere would never be enough.

What was she going to do now? He was her roommate, for crying out loud. She would see him every day without fail and fall more and more in love with him.

With a groan, she banged her head against the elevator doors. As if awaiting that cue, the lift stopped and rattled open. No one was in the hallway, thank goodness.

More out of habit than need, she straightened the neckline of her dress and started toward her office.

Her heels tapping along the tile corridor, her mind raced with indecision. What should she do? Tell Daniel the truth and risk rejection? Lie and say she wasn't interested so would he please not kiss her anymore? Admit her feelings? Find another flat?

One by one she examined each idea and tossed it aside. There was no answer to her dilemma.

For years, she'd kept an arm's length from every man. Now, in the space of a short few weeks, Daniel had crowded past her guard and seeped into her heart. She couldn't escape that fact any more than she could escape him. She wanted to be with him. She wanted to be kissed and held and loved again.

Okay. There was her answer. Not a perfect solution, but one she could live with. She could enjoy his company, accept his kisses, but make her intentions clear—she would never agree to an affair. That was the only way she could keep her sanity and also keep her secret. When he tired of her and moved on, she would survive. She always had.

As she passed the accounting office raised voices caught her attention. She slowed to a stop, listening, relieved to focus on something besides her tumultuous emotional state.

"Don't worry about it," Dominic was saying, his tone strained. "I can take care of the problem by Friday."

A voice she didn't recognize muttered something in reply. She couldn't make out the words, but the tone was tense. Curiosity lifted the hairs on the back of her neck.

What was going on in there?

She moved closer but noise from the kitchen blotted out the conversation. She caught bits and pieces, a word here and there, and, after a few minutes of unsuccessful eavesdropping, began to feel silly. If she wanted to know what was going on, she could ask, not stand in the hall lurking like a criminal. Ever since John had questioned her about a vendor transaction she'd made from her flat, she'd been suspicious of everyone and everything. Add Daniel's confirmation that her name had come up as one having access and she was jumping at shadows.

She went into her office and waited until she heard

the door of the accounting office open. Then she stepped back into the hallway.

Dominic stood in the entry of his office watching the pair depart. He ran a finger beneath his shirt collar and took a deep breath.

"Dominic."

He whirled around, noticing her for the first time. "Stephanie, hullo. You startled me."

"I thought I heard angry voices. Who were those men?"

His eyes, so like Daniel's and yet so different, shifted toward the back door. "Those men? Mr Sandusky and Mr Richardson?"

He seemed reluctant to tell her more, but she remained silent, waiting. Finally, Dominic gave a short laugh and rubbed a hand over his head. Daniel had that same habit, but the effect was quite different on a balding pate. "That wasn't arguing. That was debate over a very important topic. My brother."

Now she was taken by surprise. "Daniel?" What did he have to do with this?

"Sandusky and Richardson are investors. I'm trying to convince them that Dan's water ventures could eventually be nice moneymakers for their group."

And here she'd been thinking bad thoughts. "What a wonderful thing to do, Dominic. Daniel will be touched."

A modest blush stained his cheeks. "He's my twin. I want the best for him. And if sweetening up some business investors will help, I'll do it."

"You really should tell him. He has videos, photos, statistics, all kinds of information that could seal the deal."

"No. No. Not yet." He stood up straighter, fidgeted with

his tie. "I'd rather wait until they've committed. I don't want Daniel disappointed if they don't come on board."

"Oh, I see." And she did. She also felt terrible for the ugly doubts that had popped into her head. "Well, let me know if I can be of any help. Daniel will be thrilled by this."

Then she went inside her office and shut the door.

Poor, sweet Dominic.

All day she'd been worrying about the tampered accounts and trying to pinpoint suspects. In hopes of affirming her own innocence, she'd begun to wonder about Dominic.

The problem had begun shortly after Dominic came to work for the restaurants. But that was all the so-called evidence she had. Well, except for the two times she'd walked into his office unannounced and seen him scramble to log off the computer.

She chided her runaway imagination. The guy was probably looking at sexy pictures and was embarrassed at being caught. She had no business thinking the worst of Daniel's brother.

Thank goodness, she hadn't said anything. An unfounded accusation could alienate both John and Daniel. Worse yet, it could hurt them. And the last thing she ever wanted to do was hurt her boss or the man she was falling in love with.

But someone was responsible. If she wasn't guilty, and Dominic wasn't guilty, it could very well be, as John feared, someone else in the family. But who?

CHAPTER SEVEN

LIFE was starting to go his way.

Daniel softly punched a fist into his palm, excited about the new agreement with AquaSphere Associates. Even the cloudy day couldn't dampen his enthusiasm.

He stopped in the restaurant's back doorway to scratch the kitten under the chin.

Stephanie had been right. Meeting with his father's business contacts had resulted in the first of what should be many more contracts for his fledgling company.

For all his reluctance to attend the lunch meeting, Daniel had to admit his father seemed genuinely committed to helping him. The issue still made him uneasy. A lifetime of neglect couldn't be made up in weeks, and money wouldn't fix the hurt of having no boyhood father. He wasn't sure what to feel for John. One thing for certain, trust had to be earned. And the jury was still out on that one.

The kitten arched her back and rubbed against his calf as he walked away, leaving stray hairs on his dark trousers. It had been a long time since he'd dressed in a suit and tie. He didn't much care for the discomfort, but the new haircut seemed to demand more conservative attire.

His thoughts drifted pleasantly from the meeting to the afternoon Stephanie had trimmed his hair. He ran a hand over his head, grinning at the memory. Not surprisingly, she'd done a good job of taming his unruly locks, at least to some degree. A perfectionist like her wouldn't have offered if she wasn't sure of the outcome.

It was the minutes after the haircut that stayed with him, though. That first kiss was imprinted on his mind as permanently as a tattoo. At the time, he'd thought it was the only kiss he'd ever get, but she'd surprised him the next day by kissing him. Not on the cheek as she'd done before, but on the lips, proving that she'd forgiven whatever wrong he'd done.

He didn't know why that pleased him so much, all things considered.

Now that she didn't jump every time he came near, Stephanie was great company. She was intellectually stimulating, witty, and generous to a fault. He knew she befriended her staff almost to excess, loaning money, listening to sob stories, filling in when someone needed time off. But she was also generous to him in ways that boggled his already confused thought processes. Without his knowledge, she'd spent hours developing a PowerPoint presentation from his slides. The exceptional work had most certainly made the difference in today's meeting.

If that wasn't enough to get any man thinking about her, she was also the most coolly gorgeous thing he'd ever seen. He could deal with that. But living under the same roof with a woman who stopped at kisses was driving him quite mad. And she would never agree to the only kind of relationship he could give, a physical one. He wished he had more to offer, but he didn't.

Ah, well, kisses were better than nothing.

Maybe he'd ask her to celebrate today's success with him. Perhaps take her to a football match, or they could head to the West End for dinner and a play. Stephanie would like that, he was sure, and he did own a decent suit now.

Happy and full of excess energy, he decided to take the stairway up to the flat. Pounding the steps two at a time, he reached the top without breaking a sweat.

Stereo music blasted through the glass balcony doors. Classic hard rock. Daniel laughed as he stepped inside the living room. The insistent, driving sound was so unlike the smooth jazz Stephanie preferred in the restaurant.

Only slightly winded, he drew in a deep breath. Stephanie's perfume swamped him.

Yes, it was a good day. A good, good day.

"Stephanie," he called, but wasn't surprised when she didn't answer. Superman couldn't hear over that music.

He followed the sound down the hall, thinking to knock on her bedroom door until she heard him.

When he saw that her door was already open, he slowed.

And then he froze.

Back to him, she stood at the closet, rifling through a rack of clothes encased in clear plastic cleaner bags. Her long wavy hair was piled on top of her head with the usual stray curls tumbling down. Tall, slim, and lithe, the beautiful redhead was nude.

But it wasn't the nakedness that had his heart slamming against his ribcage with the force of a freight train.

It was the scars.

From shoulder blades to mid-thigh, long, white scars marred the perfection of an otherwise beautiful body.

Daniel rocked back. What on earth—?

He stood in the dim hallway for several more stunned moments before realizing he had to get away. He couldn't let her catch him here, not like this, not when his face must register the storm raging inside.

Wheeling on the heels of his shiny new shoes, Daniel raced out of the flat and thundered down the stairs. Right now, he couldn't face anyone. He needed time alone to assess what he'd just witnessed.

The alleyway was thankfully empty except for rubbish bins, the kitten, and an illegally parked car. Weak in the knees and breathless, he leaned against the brick wall at the back of the restaurant and closed his eyes. The image of Stephanie's battered skin arose like a bad dream.

What had happened? Fire? A car crash?

He saw the scars again, the long, slashing stripes that lay like ritualistic lashes across her entire backside.

Ritualistic lashes.

As if he'd been slammed in the gut with a sledgehammer, all the air whooshed out of him.

Oh, my God.

A trembling started down his soul. He fought the tide of emotion, scared of what it meant. Pity. This must be pity. And rage. He had never been so angry. Not at his mother. Not at John. Not even at the inhuman conditions he had witnessed in the course of his work.

Some vile, evil maniac had intentionally beaten Stephanie until she was terribly, irreconcilably scarred. Not once, not even twice, but many times in a ritual of abuse.

Their conversation in the restaurant came back to him, sharp and in focus, making sense now. When she'd said her boyfriend had hurt her badly, he'd suspected violence, but this was unfathomable. Only a monster could have done this.

Why had she stayed with him? Why had she let this happen, not once but many times? Had she been controlled by him in some way? Threatened and afraid? Was this why she'd come to England? To escape a maniac?

His temples throbbed with a dozen questions he couldn't ask. Stephanie didn't want him to know. She'd be destroyed if she thought he had discovered her secret.

The scars explained so much. The reasons she had avoided physical contact with him, the fear in her eyes until he'd finally proven himself trustworthy. Even the elegant dresses that showed so little skin now made sense.

Stephanie's wariness wasn't from a cold heart. It was self-preservation.

He squeezed his eyes shut against the onslaught of emotion rising up inside him, swallowed the vile sickness in his throat. His poor, beautiful, broken Stephanie.

The devil who had committed this heinous crime deserved to die. And Daniel would have gladly done the deed without a blink of remorse.

* * *

Daniel walked the streets of Kensington for more than two hours before returning to the restaurant. Long shadows of evening fell across the alley. The kitten greeted him as usual. This time he picked her up and rubbed his face against her fur, soaking in the purring comfort before opening the back door.

His shirt was rumpled and untucked. His shoes were now scuffed and dirty. He'd long since shoved the silk tie into a pocket and loosened the top shirt button.

The smells emanating from inside the Bella Lucia made his stomach growl. To a man who hadn't eaten since lunch, the scent of Italian food was pure heaven—ironic considering how sick he'd felt earlier.

The need to talk drove him to stop at Dominic's office, but his brother had already gone home to Alice and the kids. The knowledge that his twin had someone to go home to struck Daniel with a loneliness he seldom experienced. He'd never know that pleasure of family, never have someone to share his life and troubles.

The moment he walked into the dining room, he spotted Stephanie. His gut clenched.

Cool and smooth as the terracotta tile beneath her feet, Stephanie moved from table to table, dropping a warm greeting, a welcoming smile, a complimentary bottle of wine. The restaurant pulsed around her with the beat of unobtrusive jazz, trendy, chic, a respite from the busy streets outside.

No one would ever guess the pain and betrayal she'd lived through.

His admiration edged upward. She'd suffered far

more than he ever had and yet she'd chosen not to wither, but to bloom.

Out of sight of customers, Daniel leaned in the doorway, watching her, the perfect manager, perfectly groomed, perfectly poised, perfect in every way except for the terrible sorrow she hid from the world.

Tenderness threatened to choke him.

Regardless of what had happened to her, Stephanie had made a success of her life. She went right on caring about the people around her, nurturing those in need, giving, loving.

And unless he'd missed something, she had no one in her life to reciprocate. Who tended her when she was sick? Held her when she cried?

With a sigh, Daniel wondered if life would have been different if he'd ever learned to love someone other than himself. But no matter. He hadn't. His heart was as empty as the devil's soul, whether he liked it or not. He wasn't the kind of man Stephanie needed. He wasn't the kind of man any woman needed for more than a night or two, an admission that left him emptier than ever.

Stephanie disappeared into the cloakroom. Unfamiliar tenderness crowding his better judgment, Daniel pushed away from the wall and followed.

He eased up behind her and placed a kiss on the back of her neck.

"All work and no play—"

Stephanie spun around. Her skin tingled from the featherlike touch of Daniel's lips, from his warm breath on her skin. Since the first time they'd kissed and she'd realized she loved him, something had broken loose inside her. Though she would eventually pay with a broken heart, she hungered for the touch of another human being. But not just anyone. Daniel.

"I wondered where you were. How did things go today?"

"Great." He told her about the contract, but his mind seemed somewhere else. "I need someone to celebrate with me. How about you?"

A celebration with Daniel sounded lovely. "I'm working."

He took her hands and pulled her toward him. The usual mischief danced in his eyes, but tonight she saw something else in those blue depths that she couldn't quite define.

"So," he said as he nuzzled her temple. "These excellent employees of yours can't finish the evening without you?"

Stephanie resisted the longing to lean closer and soak him up like the dry sponge of need she was. "Of course they can."

"Good." He stepped back, still holding her hands in his warm, calloused grip. "Grab your coat and let's go. I'll take you anywhere you choose. Say the word and I'll even put the cursed tie back on."

She laughed. "This is your celebration."

"Right. So indulge me. You choose."

He stroked a finger along her cheek, smiling at her in the strangest way. There it was again, that subtle difference, as though he really cared about what she wanted.

"You're in an unusual mood."

"Nothing unusual about taking my favorite lady out for a good time."

His favorite lady? Where had that come from?

He ushered her from the cloakroom, skirting around the diners to slip out the front door.

"I need to let Sheila know I'm leaving," Stephanie protested.

"Call her from the flat." Without warning, he backed her against the wall. On the streets, traffic pulsed and somewhere a car honked, but the air around the two of them grew silent. That gentle, questioning expression appeared on Daniel's face again. Then his lips covered hers with such exquisite tenderness Stephanie almost felt loved.

What in the world was going on with him tonight?

Whatever was going on didn't relent in the days to come.

On a blustery afternoon when November had shortened the days and the sky threatened a cold rain, Stephanie donned slacks and sweater for yet another outing with the indefatigable Daniel. The man had more energy than an electric company. He could spend the morning schmoozing clients, visiting job sites, and frequently working himself into a dirty, sweaty mess, then come breezing in to whisk her away from the restaurant for a few hours of adventure. Invariably, she protested out of duty to her job, but her protests grew weaker with every soft kiss and tender caress. She was helpless to turn down these special moments with the new, solicitous Daniel.

Coat and gloves in hand, she met him in the living room. All cleaned up in blue jeans and a turquoise sweater that turned his eyes to jewels, he helped her into her long leather coat. When he began to button it up with his large, competent fingers, a swell of pure pleasure filled Stephanie to the point of no return.

Head bent, a wayward lock of his dark hair fell forward. Stephanie pushed it away, then let her fingers drift down to the warm, whisker-rough curve of his cheek.

Lord, she loved this man.

"All done." But he didn't step back. Instead, he took her scarf, draped it around her neck and used the soft flannel to bring her face in line with his. The whisper of his breath, minty and fresh, kissed her lips. "Ready, then?"

"Ready." She was as breathless as if she'd run six flights of stairs.

Hand holding hers, he led the way to the elevator.

"Where are you kidnapping me to?" she asked when they were inside the lift.

He pressed the floor indicator and, with a wicked grin that set her heart thudding, said, "Secret."

He'd told her only that they wouldn't be back until late and she should dress casually. A twinge of guilt said she shouldn't be gone during the dinner rush, but John had told her more than once lately that she worked too much and should take more time off. She wondered if Daniel had anything to do with that.

"Let me check in with Sheila and make sure everything is running smoothly before we go."

Still grinning in that wicked, wicked manner, he backed her against the metal wall. "No."

She pushed at his chest. "I can't enjoy myself unless I'm sure everything is covered."

Sighing an overly dramatic martyr's sigh, Daniel slumped. "Woman, have you never in your life done anything irresponsible?"

On tiptoe, she kissed him. "Humor me. I might be worth it."

"Kiss me again and I'll believe you."

She obliged, and Daniel, the naughty man, deepened the kiss, holding it while the elevator pinged open and then closed again.

"Daniel!" Stephanie cried when he finally let her come up for air. Something had definitely come over him tonight.

"What?" His handsome face was a study in innocence.

She whacked him playfully on the arm. "Are we going to spend the entire evening in this elevator?"

He cocked his head as if giving the idea serious thought. "Can't beat the privacy. Let's do it."

Doing it would be wonderful, but Stephanie couldn't ever go there again. Not even with Daniel. She leaned around him and pushed the down button.

"Spoilsport." But he draped an arm around her waist and snuggled her close, nuzzling her neck in the seconds from her flat to the restaurant.

"You're making this very difficult."

"That's the plan."

When they finally exited the elevator, laughing like two sneaking teenagers, Stephanie felt lighter and happier than she had since the day she'd left Denver.

With Daniel's hand at her back in the most protective way, they went into the restaurant, spoke briefly to the competent Sheila, and then retraced their steps to the back door.

"We could use the front entrance, you know," Stephanie said.

"What about the motorcycle I have waiting?"

"You do not," she said, but, knowing Daniel as she did, he probably did.

His eyes gleamed with mischief. "Try me."

A thrill of excitement raced along Stephanie's spine. She couldn't think of anything more wonderful than riding behind Daniel, her arms around his waist as the cold wind whipped her hair and stung her cheeks.

He paused outside Dominic's office and reached inside his coat pocket to extract a small box. "Let me drop this off first. Dominic's eldest is having a birthday."

Before Stephanie could comment on his thoughtfulness, Daniel pushed the door open. Two men whirled around. Anger sizzled from them as palpable and menacing as a nest of vipers.

Stephanie's breath froze in her throat. The investors were back and none too happy. Dominic sat behind the desk perspiring profusely.

She didn't know what was going on, but something was badly wrong. The tension in the room was thick enough to choke an elephant.

Daniel's hands fisted at his side. He looked from his brother to the two men. "Is there a problem?"

His tone was tough and protective, leaving no doubt about whose side he was on.

A pair of the hardest, coldest eyes she'd ever seen glared back. "No problem at all." The reptilian glance shifted to Dominic. "Isn't that right, Dom?"

Dominic pushed up from the squeaky chair. Stephanie couldn't help noticing a tremble in his hands. "Everything is fine. Just a bit of unfinished business." He hustled around the desk to usher the two men to the door. "I'll call you tomorrow about that project. You have my word."

Daniel looked at Stephanie and murmured, "What's going on?"

She lifted her shoulders, afraid he wouldn't appreciate her thoughts.

The rumble of voices in the hall told her that Dominic's unfinished business was quite a serious topic.

When Dominic returned to the office visibly shaken, Daniel asked, "What was that all about? Who were those guys?"

"Old friends." His face was pale. "No one you know."

Now Stephanie knew he was lying. The ugly suspicion rose again, this time with enough strength to give the doubts validity. Dominic wasn't soliciting investors for his brother's business. He was up to no good. He had to be. Otherwise, why behave so strangely and lie so blatantly?

This time, Stephanie had no choice. She had to inform John that something was not right with the accountant. Maybe he wasn't embezzling funds, but something was definitely amiss.

Stephanie glanced at Daniel, her heart sinking lower than the Alaskan sun. She was about to accuse his brother of a crime.

He was going to hate her for this.

CHAPTER EIGHT

"LIKE it?" Daniel shouted over one shoulder, his voice yanked away by the force of wind and speed.

Stephanie leaned forward, mouth all but touching Daniel's ear. "It's wonderful."

The motorcycle sped through the streets and alleys of London, dodging in and out of places they probably shouldn't have ridden. But Daniel, confident and competent, had no fear. With him in control Stephanie didn't either. Hands locked over the smooth, supple leather of his jacket, she reveled in the energy racing through her bloodstream. For the first time in a long time, she felt carefree and alive.

She could have ridden for ever and been happy, but Daniel slowed and pulled into a parking bay.

"We're going to be tourists tonight," he said, helping her off the bike.

"Like this?" She shook her hair out, knowing she looked wild and wind-kissed.

"You're beautiful." Daniel bent to kiss her nose. "But your nose is cold."

She tiptoed up and returned the kiss. "So is yours."

He growled deep in his throat and made a teasing grab for her. With a squeal, she jumped back, stumbled and was quickly righted by his strong hands.

"Careful there. We have lots of walking to do."

Pulse tripping, more from Daniel's touch than the near fall, Stephanie slipped her hand into his. "Where are we headed?"

"There." He pointed upward at the huge, rotating London Eye. "And then other places."

Even this late in the fall, the area along the South Bank of the Thames was alive with visitors, the smells and sounds almost carnival-like. They bought tickets, joined the growing line, and boarded an enclosed glass pod of the giant observation wheel. Buildings and people grew tiny as the Eye slowly ascended.

"I feel like I'm inside a bubble," she said.

Daniel smiled his reply and moved them closer to the window. Other visitors sharing the pod oohed and ahhed, pointing out landmarks as the wheel continued its climb.

A little boy with a posh accent carried on a running commentary to his parents as various sites came into view. Daniel shrugged and stuffed his guidebook into a pocket.

"Nothing like a personal tour," he muttered against her temple.

For Stephanie, the landmarks weren't the important part of the ride. Being with Daniel was. Yet, the panorama was breathtaking.

Through a moisture-smeared veil, she glimpsed London spread in every direction around the mighty river. In the west, the sun was setting. Though the fog and haze obscured the sunset, rays of diffused light penetrated just enough to cast a glorious glow over the city.

The South Bank, a cultural Mecca for art, music and theatre, was a place she'd been wanting to visit since coming to London, but had never had the time. She was glad. Seeing the area with Daniel made it even more special.

Positioned behind her, her favorite barbarian rested his chin atop her head and pulled her back against him. Through her coat she felt the press of his jacket zipper, the mold of his muscled chest and belly, and the strength of his arms lightly bracketing her waist, and marveled at how safe she felt. She, who never felt safe in a man's arms, wanted to stay here for ever, loving him always as she did this moment.

She closed her eyes, the panorama briefly forgotten, and focused on the essence of Daniel. He smelled of leather and fresh air and that manly scent that was uniquely his. Though a dozen or so other people occupied the pod, Stephanie felt as if they were the only two people around. Something magical had happened when he'd come into her life, as if the thick miasma of fear and distrust had blown away in the fresh breeze of a man without false motives.

She knew where she stood with him. He'd made no secret that they could never be more than they were now, a fact that both comforted and seared. Comforted because he would never see the scars and be repelled. Seared because she loved him and knew these moments with him could not last.

The quiet burr of his voice forced her eyes open.

"According to our worthy guide," he said wryly, "we can spy Buckingham Palace right over there." He dipped closer, his cheek to hers, and pointed in the general direction.

The touch of his skin against hers was electric. She turned to face him, resisted the urge to kiss the corner of that sexy mouth. "I think we could see the entire city if the weather was clear."

"The view from right here is even lovelier." As if he wanted to memorize every feature, Daniel scanned her face.

"Why, Mr Stephens, are you trying to flatter me into another late-night trip for cheesecake and chocolate sauce?"

"Is it working?"

"Could be," she answered and was rewarded with a quick flash of white teeth against his dark skin.

And then the rest of the trip around the wheel was lost as they focused on each other instead of the London skyline. For Stephanie those moments staring into Daniel's handsome face defined the evening. Inside their own glass bubble, a real romance with the man she had fallen in love with actually seemed possible.

When the ride ended, they strolled the promenade along the waterfront, stopping to watch the cruise ships pass. Darkness had come and streetlamps illuminated the tree-lined path and reflected off the river's edge in a dance of shadows and light.

"It's a long walk around," Daniel said when she opted to walk to the Millennium Bridge.

"I don't mind." The longer they walked, the longer she

would be with him, alone and having fun. And the longer she could pretend they had something special together.

"We can hire a cab back to the bike."

"Or walk." Like a happy child, she wrapped her arms around herself and spun around in a circle. "This is so awesome."

Daniel caught up to her, grabbed her hands and whirled her again. "I thought you would fret over the restaurant all night."

"Shh. Don't tell a soul. I'm relieved to be away for a while." The Bella Lucia didn't worry her, but she couldn't get Dominic, and the coming conversation with John, off her mind. Daniel hadn't said a word more about the incident in the office, but he had to be concerned as well. Even if Dominic hadn't taken the money, something was not quite right with Daniel's twin.

She stopped spinning and the open lapels of her long coat swished against her boot tops. "What do you think is going on with Dominic?"

Daniel grew serious. "I think he may be in trouble, though he doesn't confide in me the way he once did."

"No guesses? No twin's intuition?"

He frowned, deep furrows in his sun-bronzed brow. "None."

She wanted to ask if he thought his brother would embezzle money, but feared Daniel would take offense. And the last thing she wanted tonight was to spoil the magical evening.

"It worries you. I shouldn't have brought it up." They started walking again. "Change of subject. Tell me about your work today. About the projects. What's happening?"

"One of the reasons for my good mood." He seemed relieved to sidestep the topic of his brother. "Today I hired two water technicians and another engineer to help carry the load on all the waste-water management projects I've taken on. Plus, I have a meeting set up next week with Lord Rathington."

She blinked up at him. "Should I be impressed?"

"Very." Daniel's proud smile pushed the Dominic dilemma to the back of her mind. "The man owns half of Britain, including WS Associates, the consulting firm that can make or break an upstart company like mine. And, rumor has it, he's made a few safaris to Africa."

"Ah."

"Exactly. He seldom meets personally with anyone, but he's agreed to see me."

Stephanie smiled. "You are the most amazing man to have achieved all this since coming to London."

He laughed. "You give me too much credit. I'm sure my father had something to do with it."

"Be that as it may, I think you're amazing, and I'm proud of you."

"Keep talking. You're good for my ego."

She was in the process of forming a snappy come-back when they rounded a curve in the river and a glorious display of lights blazed in the darkness.

"Is that St Paul's?" Stephanie stared in wonder at the elegant old cathedral.

"Glorious, isn't it?"

"I had no idea it was this impressive. I suppose it's closed at this time of night?" she asked, hoping.

"I'm afraid so. But there *is* something here in the neighborhood I want to show you."

Her disappointment at not seeing the interior of St Paul's turned to curiosity. There were so many landmarks in this section of London, she wondered what he could have in mind. Perhaps the Globe? Or the Tate Modern? He knew she loved contemporary art. He'd even teased her about it when she'd said she hated the masters but loved the abstract and avant-garde. Of course, she hadn't told him why she despised those classic paintings. Another secret better kept.

Instead of the Tate, however, he turned down a side street toward a closed and darkened business section.

"Where are we going?"

"You'll see," he said mysteriously, suppressed excitement in every word.

"Now I really am curious."

Boots echoing along the quiet street, Daniel stopped in front of a lovely older brick office building.

"Here we are. She has character, don't you think?"

"Yes. But exactly who is she?"

"*She* is the office space I leased today for Stephens International Water Design."

"Daniel! Oh, my goodness." She didn't know whether to laugh or cry. He looked so proud and so much like a small boy wanting approval.

She threw her arms around him in an enthusiastic embrace. "This is marvelous. A real office. Can we go in? Please."

Her reaction clearly thrilled him. He threw his head back and laughed. "Whatever the lady desires."

She desired, all right, something far more precious than a tour of an office building. But seeing Daniel happy was enough for now.

Inside the small but pleasant office space, Daniel stood with hands on hips waiting for her to comment.

"I can see a pair of plush chairs here along this wall, blue, I think," she said, moving around the room as decorating images flashed in her head. "And a nice wall grouping above them. Perhaps a black and white photo display of some of your projects. And the desk will go here. A very modern computer desk and—"

Daniel caught her in mid-sentence and spun her around. "You're a special woman, Stephanie."

Her heart caught in her throat. "Because I like to decorate?"

His chuckle raised warm goose bumps on her arms. "Because I needed you to approve."

Was that uncertainty? In a man as confident and strong as Daniel?

"This office is perfect. And what better place for a water-project engineer than along the shores of the Thames?"

"I knew you'd appreciate the symbolism."

Hand in hand, they took a brief tour of the office, then made their way back out on the street. All the way to the Millennium Bridge, Daniel talked nonstop about his plans and ideas for the fledgling business.

"You will succeed beyond your wildest dreams, Daniel," she said when he expressed a concern to the contrary. "I believe that with all my heart."

The long, water-washed pedestrian bridge stretched across the river and welcomed strolling couples. Stephanie and Daniel walked to the center and stopped to look down at the river below.

Lights from the shore gleamed on the water, and fog twisted and smeared the panorama into an impressionistic painting. Gentle music from a passing cruise ship wafted up to them. With a half-smile that made her pulse race, Daniel inclined his head.

"Dance?"

A few other strollers passed by, but Stephanie paid them no mind. She lifted the edge of her long coat and dipped a curtsey, then stepped into Daniel's beloved arms. For a few glorious minutes while the boat hovered nearby, they swayed and swirled on the pedestrian bridge. Resting her cheek in the crook of his neck, she reveled in the scent of his skin and delighted in the beat of his heart echoing hers.

Could he be feeling the same thing she was? This incredible surge of joy, this new willingness to be vulnerable to another person regardless of the past? Her heart swelled with the hope that both of them could lay aside their hurts and move forward together. She loved him. Dared she admit her feelings?

Everything he did tonight spoke of caring, but he claimed to have no love to give. With each passing moment in his company, Stephanie found that harder and harder to believe. If this continued, she would have to tell him.

But not tonight. She couldn't chance shattering the lovely fantasy of tonight. Here in Daniel's arms along the bank of the Thames, she could pretend that he loved her, too.

"Telephone call, Stephanie. The man says it's very important."

The evening rush was on and the restaurant was alive with trendy Londoners. Stephanie didn't mind. She was still walking on air from the incredible date with Daniel the evening before.

"Okay, thanks, Sheila."

She scribbled "zucchini" on a notepad beside the kitchen door, then caught herself and wrote "courgette" instead. The dish had come back to the kitchen uneaten on several plates. And whether she called the vegetable courgette or zucchini, less than marvelous food was not acceptable in her restaurant.

"He's calling long distance. From Colorado."

Her pen clattered to the tile.

"Colorado?" Was that squeaky sound coming from her? "Tell the waiting staff to downplay the courgette and recommend the potato-aubergine tart as an alternative. I'll be right back."

With a heavy dread, Stephanie went into her office, closing the door behind her. She took several long, steadying breaths, then punched the hold button.

"Stephanie Ellison speaking."

She braced herself for the horrid voice.

"Miss Ellison?" Relief shimmied through her. It wasn't him. "George Howard Whittier here. I hope I haven't caught you at a bad time."

Her stepfather's law partner. She glanced up at the clock, calculating the time in Colorado. Afternoon, if she figured correctly, though the sun had set in London. "Is something wrong?"

"I'm sorry to break the news so abruptly, but I've had difficulty tracking your whereabouts. I do hope you're not alone." Gentlemanly hesitation hummed across the ocean.

"What is it, Mr Whittier?"

"My dear, your father passed away two weeks ago."

Stephanie dropped the telephone and slithered to the floor.

Daniel tossed restlessly in his bed. He'd had a bad feeling all day, a kind of premonition that something was amiss. In the sometimes dangerous situations he had been in while working abroad, he'd learned to trust his gut instincts. The simplest clue, such as a sudden hush of animal sounds in the darkness, often meant trouble ahead.

Tonight he felt that same hush brooding over the flat. Stephanie had come in an hour ago, claiming exhaustion, and had gone straight to bed. He knew the restaurant had been hopping tonight, but he was disappointed. He looked forward to the evenings when they had time to talk.

All day, she'd been on his mind. Her sweetness, her scent, the taste of her skin. When he'd shown her his future office space, she'd reacted just as he'd hoped, with the same excitement he'd experienced when he'd signed the lease.

He flopped over on the firm mattress and punched his pillow into a fluffier lump. If the noise wouldn't bother Stephanie he'd get up and work on the new monitoring design for flood control in North Yorkshire.

If she weren't so tired, he'd wake her and they'd sneak down to the kitchen for a midnight snack.

He slammed the pillow again. Might as well admit, Stephens, you're miffed. After last night when they'd had such a great time, he had expected a repeat performance or, at least, a recap. There had been that moment on the bridge when they'd danced and the world had seemed to fade away, leaving only the two of them. He relished the idea of being alone with her, frequently and for long periods.

He sat up, feet over the side of the bed, and shoved five fingers through the top of his hair. What was happening to him? His mind should be on work and water and fund-raising. Those things were his life. A woman was only a passing fancy, but Stephanie no longer fit his carefully structured view of women.

Frustrated, he flopped backwards on the bed and lay staring at the shadows dancing on the ceiling.

A sharp cry yanked him up again.

"Stephanie?" he called, knowing she couldn't hear from this far away. He got up and opened his bedroom door. A scream pierced the night. Whimpering sobs began. And then a terrible pleading.

"No. Please. No."

Hair rose on his arms.

He'd heard her nightmares when he'd first arrived and had done nothing. In time, the bad dreams had subsided. But now he couldn't stay away. Not after he'd seen the scars.

Heart thundering, he rushed into her bedroom.

"Stephanie. Love. Wake up."

Eyes accustomed to the darkness, he could see her, feel her thrashing in agony. Without a second thought, Daniel climbed onto the bed and pulled her into his arms.

"No. Please." She fought him like a wild thing, but his strength was far greater—just as someone else's had been. An awful sick lump formed in his throat.

"Stephanie. Love. It's Daniel. Wake up. You're safe. You're safe." He held fast, pressing her face into his naked shoulder until she went limp against him, and he knew she had awakened.

Her body trembled while Daniel crooned meaningless words of comfort against her hair. Even sweat-soaked, she smelled of exotic flowers.

When at last she quieted, he stroked the damp hair from her face and kissed her forehead. "Tell me."

She shook her head and shrank back as if only now aware that they were in a bed together. "A nightmare."

That was obvious. "About?" he urged as gently as he knew how.

Using the sheet for a tissue, she dabbed her damp eyes, then drew in a long, shuddering breath. "Something happened tonight. A phone call from my family's attorney."

Daniel waited, saying nothing, but trying to put the two events together.

"My father died two weeks ago." The words came out flat and wooden. "And I didn't even know."

For Daniel, missing his father's funeral wouldn't have mattered even a month ago, but now that family had intruded into his life he knew he would care if something happened to John. He didn't want to care and wasn't about to let John know as much, but he would. Stephanie hadn't been home for her own father's funeral. Understandable that news of his death would set off a bad dream.

"I'm sorry, love. Truly." He wanted to hold her, but

she seemed not to want that, so he settled for touching the back of her cheek with his knuckles.

"I have to go to Colorado," she whispered, "and settle the estate."

"So soon?" Daniel flipped on the bedside lamp.

Stephanie's eyes were red and wild as she blinked against the sudden flood of light.

"Yes. Now. Tomorrow." Her hands began to pick and twist at the sheet in a way that Daniel recognized as deep anxiety.

"Is it that urgent?"

"I don't want to go back, but I have to."

A quiver of worry intruded. "Is he still there? Your ex?"

"Brett?" She looked bewildered. "No. No. Not anymore."

He felt a measure of relief. If the monster who'd abused her wasn't there, she'd be safe.

She shoved off the bed. Silk pajamas whispered against her skin. She paced to the window and back. The trembling started again and Daniel wasn't sure what she needed.

He offered all he could. "You've had terrible news. You're distraught. Come here. Let me hold you."

As if he were the lifeboat in a stormy ocean, she fell upon him, knocking him onto his back. He took her with him.

Her wild tangle of curls fell across his face. He pushed them aside, trying to read her expression, to understand what she was feeling.

"Come with me, Daniel," she murmured, the request urgent, almost frantic. "I can't do this alone."

"Love." Beyond that, he was at a loss. The old fear rose up. What was she asking?

"Please, Daniel. I need you beside me. I need your strength. I love you. You have to know that by now. And I need you with me. I can't get through this alone."

Daniel stiffened. She loved him?

Oh, no.

Stephanie's warm, slender body lay atop his and yet he had no sexual urgings, just the terrible need to run. He was a coward of the worst kind, but the word love scared him out of his mind.

"Stephanie, sweetheart. Listen to me." He rolled them to the side so they lay face-to-face. Her stormy sea eyes were wild and distraught. "You don't love me. You can't."

He wasn't lovable. And he had no love in him. Hadn't he told her as much?

"But I do," she whispered. "I didn't mean to. I didn't want to. But I love you."

Daniel released a groan of dismay. What had he done? Stephanie needed far more than he had to give. She deserved far more than a man with no heart, no soul.

He squeezed his eyes closed against the onslaught of despair. No matter what he did now, she would be hurt even more than she already was.

The best thing he could do for both of them was get away. He sat up, putting distance between them. If he touched her much longer, he'd do something stupid. She didn't deserve the kind of misery a life with him would bring. He was too empty. He had nothing to give her. Nothing.

"We agreed early on that neither of us wanted emotional commitment." He couldn't look at her. "You can't love me, Stephanie." His own mother hadn't. How could she? "I can't love you. I don't know how. I don't have it in me."

She touched his bare arm. "You're wrong. You have so much love, it scares you."

He shook his head. She didn't understand. He didn't expect her to.

"Don't you see, Daniel? A man who gives his entire life to improve life for others has plenty of love. You're afraid. That's all. So was I, but you're not like him."

She was afraid of loving, too, and now he'd ruined her for good. She would never chance letting another through her force field of protection.

"I'm sorry, Stephanie. Truly." She'd never know how sorry.

"Go with me, Daniel. No strings. I can't do this alone."

But she loved him and love always expected something in return.

"The meeting with Lord Rathington," he said feebly.

Drawing the sheet up like a coat of armor, she sat up straighter in the center of the bed. Her expression went cool, her body still as stone. "Of course. How thoughtless of me. You can't miss that."

He stood like the stunned fool he was, wishing he had something more to give her. Something that mattered. In the end, he said the only thing he could. "I'll move my things into the new office while you're gone."

Red-eyed and flushed, she nodded with the regal grace of a queen. "I think that's best."

She was right. It was for the best. He had nothing to

offer her, and prolonging the relationship would serve no good purpose.

Then why did he have the strongest need to crawl back onto that bed and beg her forgiveness?

CHAPTER NINE

COLORADO was as beautiful as ever. But even the majesty of the snow-covered Rockies couldn't lift the dark mood hanging over Stephanie like a London fog as she maneuvered her rental car through the streets and inclines of downtown Denver.

As much as she dreaded the days ahead of settling the family estate, the heartache of that last fight with Daniel tormented her most.

Why had she said those foolish words? Why had she tossed her heart out on that bed for him to reject? What was it about her personality that navigated toward men destined to hurt her?

And yet, Daniel was nothing like Brett or Randolph. For all his denials and sharp cynicism, Daniel cared deeply about people. And after that wonderful, magical night along the Thames, she'd even believed he cared about her.

Over and over, for the entire international flight, she'd puzzled over Daniel's behavior and called herself ten kinds of fool. She'd walked right into that opportunity for Daniel to break her heart.

But Daniel had suffered hurt, too. Somehow, from

his mother's and father's mistakes, he'd come to think of himself as unlovable and unloving. He was wrong. But Stephanie was too tired and weak to fight anymore. She wasn't even sure she had the emotional strength to face the meeting with the Ellison family lawyer.

Her grip on the steering wheel tightened as the tall glass and steel building came in sight.

Might as well admit the truth. She was scared out of her mind.

She pulled the rental car into a parking garage filled with cold air and exhaust fumes, then rode the elevator up to the eighteenth floor to the law offices of Whittier, Ellison, and Carter. The suites, ultra-conservative, just like her stepfather, occupied one end of the floor.

An immaculately groomed brunette receptionist and a security guard manned the entrance. Randolph had always been paranoid about security. To Stephanie's way of thinking, his own conscience had known he deserved to be shot.

"Stephanie Ellison to see Mr Whittier," she told the receptionist.

The action was nothing new. Even as a child, she and her mother had been expected to check in at the desk and wait their turn as if they were nothing but business appointments instead of family. Randolph Ellison had never cut her a bit of slack. Not in any way. She wasn't expecting today to be any different.

"Miss Ellison?" The brunette assessed her with an open curiosity that would have displeased her now-dead employer. Underlings were to maintain professional decorum at all times. "Mr Whittier is expecting you. I'll buzz him and you can go right in."

"I know the way, thank you." Without waiting, Stephanie pushed through the heavy double doors and knocked at the inner office marked "George H. Whittier, Attorney at Law."

"Stephanie, my dear child, come in. Come in." Mr Whittier, tall and angular in his gray business suit, came around an enormous oak-and-glass desk to greet her. As bony as he was, she expected him to rattle.

He seated them both. "You look wonderful, positively luminous. London must agree with you."

"Thank you. I'm happy there." Or she had been until she had allowed Daniel to break her heart. She ran damp palms over her royal-blue designer suit, chosen specifically to provide the confidence needed to get through this meeting. "If you don't mind, Mr Whittier, could we get down to business? I'd like to get back to England as soon as possible."

The jovial expression turned somber. "You do realize that there is a great deal to be done before the estate can be settled. I'm afraid this may take some time."

She gripped the tiny designer purse in her lap. "How long?"

"Several weeks at least. Maybe longer with the holidays coming on. Business moves much slower at this time of year."

The holidays. She'd hardly given them a thought with all that was happening in London. But here in America, business came to a near standstill from late November through the New Year.

Her stomach began to churn. How could she face dealing with Randolph's estate for more than a day or two? The nightmares had come nonstop since she'd first gotten word of his death. It was as if he had the power to reach from the grave to torment her.

"I don't want any of it, Mr Whittier. Give everything to charity."

"That's not possible, my dear. Your father made certain you couldn't do that. You see, he was very concerned about your state of mind after you went away to college."

Concerned? Yeah, right. He was concerned that she'd tell someone the truth about the powerful, respected attorney turned local politician. But she never had. She'd been too ashamed then and she was too ashamed now.

Face carefully composed, she asked, "What do I have to do?"

"Randolph set the trust up very carefully. There are stipulations regarding distribution of certain properties."

A chill circled her heart like cold fingers. "He couldn't touch the trust my mother left me, could he?" Knowing Randolph as she did, he had tried.

"No, of course not. But the bulk of the estate is in a trust of Randolph's creation. You have control, of course, but some of the holdings come with stipulations." He picked up a sheaf of papers and cleared his throat. "Your father left a letter addressed to you."

Stephanie wanted to ask him to stop calling Randolph Ellison her father. But there was another carefully preserved lie that she wasn't ready to admit to the world.

She reached for the letter and was surprised when

the attorney did not hand it over. "I'm sorry." She dropped her hand. "I thought you said it was addressed to me."

"It is. But your father instructed that I read it aloud in your presence." He shifted, clearly uncomfortable. "I know the contents, Stephanie, and I want to apologize in advance. I tried to convince Randolph not to include this, but he insisted. Just as he insisted that it be read aloud."

One last opportunity to humiliate her, no doubt.

"You have to understand," Whittier went on. "After you left, Randolph became quite bitter. I'm afraid he never got over your abandoning him after your mother's death."

Stephanie held back an angry retort. She hadn't abandoned him. No longer afraid for her mother, she'd escaped from hell. But knowing Randolph as she did, she wasn't surprised that he had become the injured party, playing her as the ungrateful, heartless daughter.

Her head began to pound, but she kept her expression empty and her voice cool and calm. "Read the letter, please."

"Very well." Whittier gave her another long look before bowing his head to the missive and beginning to read.

> My dear Stephanie, he read.
>
> Your best interest and that of your beloved mother has always been the focus of all I do. You know this is true. I never wanted anything but the best for you.

The old hypocrite. If he'd wanted her to react to that outright lie, he would be disappointed. She sat still and straight. Randolph, good lawyer that he had been, had begun his attacks gently, saving the zinger for last. She had to be ready for anything.

> Your mother and I gave you the best life possible. We raised you in the best society, with the finest education and all the material things money could buy. Yet, you never appreciated any of it. You are an ungrateful, disobedient young woman who does not deserve my generosity.

Thank you, Daddy Dearest. You always were so very, very generous with money as long as the other price was paid.

The lawyer's gray gaze flickered up to hers, a warning that the worst was yet to come. Stephanie braced herself. The cold trembling started deep in her stomach.

The letter went on for several pages of hideous vitriol until Stephanie wanted to bolt from the room and never return. But, after all she had suffered at Randolph's hands, she was not about to give him that satisfaction.

The trembling spread to her knees. Though her face blazed with humiliation, she sat straight and stiff in the armchair and waited until the diatribe ended.

Mr Whittier lay the paper aside and looked up. "Again, my apologies, Stephanie, for the remainder of this document. Would you like some refreshment, tea perhaps, before we continue?"

"No, thank you. Just get it over with. After the last few pages, I can handle anything."

She wasn't sure if that was exactly true, but she had

no choice. On the outside she remained poised. The inside raged with anger and hurt and a sick dread.

After another moment of hesitation, Whittier pushed his glasses on and finished.

> Under the circumstances, I should turn you out in the street penniless. But I am a generous man whose charity extends beyond the grave. Considering that your real father was nothing but trash who seduced your mother and left me with his bad seed, I am not surprised by your disgraceful behavior. I'm only thankful that my blood does not flow in your veins. Nevertheless, I tried to keep you from following your mother's same wanton path. But just as I forgave her, I am forgiving you.

Whittier glanced over his bifocals. "You can rest assured, my dear, that this meeting is entirely confidential. Nothing in this letter will ever leave this room."

The heat of embarrassment deepened. She swallowed past the cotton in her throat. No one outside of her mother, herself and Randolph had ever known the truth about her parentage—until now. "Thank you."

The quiver in her voice angered her. She would not let Randolph get to her, not now.

Whittier carefully folded the letter in thirds and replaced it in the vellum envelope. "I need your signature to indicate the letter was read to you. Then I must sign before a notary as proof that I followed Randolph's instructions to the letter."

"He was always thorough." Hands trembling, she dashed her signature across the indicated line. "Is this all?"

The sooner she had this settled, the sooner she could sell that house of horrors and go home to England.

"The will itself is quite straightforward. We've only to clear the house, decide on what you want done with other properties, and wait for probate. All the properties, bank accounts, and holdings are already in your name."

She stared at him, stunned. "You're kidding. After that horrible letter, he left me everything? No strings attached?"

His expression was sympathetic. "He left you everything, but Randolph always attached strings."

Of course. The loud banging inside her head intensified. "And that would be…?"

"You are to personally clean out the family home, and neither it nor the acreage around it can ever be sold as long as you live. Randolph said you would understand his reasons."

Black spots danced in front of her eyes. The devil. Oh, yes, she understood why he had done this. He knew how much she hated that house. That she never wanted to cross that threshold again. So he connived to punish her one final, lifelong time.

Daniel slapped the lift button and waited impatiently for the door to ping open.

He didn't think his week could get any worse. After supervising a job site east of the city, he'd come back to find problems with another project. Then word came that his furniture couldn't be delivered for at least a week, and now this urgent call from his brother.

His black mood deepened. Annoyed with waiting, he abandoned the lift and pounded down the stairs.

Stephanie had been gone a few days and since she'd left, his mood had been black as midnight. Nothing was going right, and he was going crazy living in that flat. If he had to sleep on his bare office floor, he was moving out.

The flat screamed Stephanie's name, her scent, her belongings. Even her art and the fastidious organization of her kitchen cabinets reminded him of her.

He couldn't sleep either, something he'd always been able to do, even under the most adverse environmental conditions. Then last night, he'd completely lost it. He'd suffered the stupid urge to crawl into Stephanie's empty bed. At the last minute, he'd camped on the floor of the living room, her pillow cradled in his arms for the entire sleepless night.

Yup. He was losing his mind.

And to top it all off, something serious was happening with his brother. In the urgent phone call just now, he'd heard fear and desperation. All Dominic would say was, "I'm in trouble, Dan. Get down here fast."

So here he was, out of breath, cranky, and worried as he entered the small accounting office.

Dominic sat at his desk, complexion gray as ashes. Their father, John, sat across from him. Daniel glanced from one to the other and back again. They were both as grim as a double murder.

He felt a protective need to stand between the two. "What's going on?" he asked.

The question was meant for Dominic, but John replied.

"For the past few weeks money has slowly disappeared from the Bella Lucia accounts."

"Yeah?" He knew that. Stephanie worried about the issue all the time. He also suspected what was coming, and the idea that his own father would accuse Dominic of stealing got his hackles up.

"Stephanie came to me with her suspicions," John said quietly.

Daniel felt as if he'd been struck by lightning. "Stephanie?"

How could she do that? Why hadn't she at least warned him?

John waved off his protestation. "Don't blame her. She didn't want to say anything, but she had to. It took a bit of work, but we finally figured out how the money was being diverted."

John's sad gaze settled on Dominic. With a start, Daniel saw the physical similarities between his fraternal twin and their father. "Your idea was both simple and brilliantly clever. Set up false service accounts into which the money, in the guise of payments, was electronically diverted from a remote location, so that any of the other people with access could be blamed. Why, son? Why would you do this?"

Eyes downcast, Dominic rested his forehead on the heel of his hand, his voice desperate. "I only meant to borrow the money. I was going to put it back, I swear." He lifted his head and looked at Daniel. "You have to believe me, Dan. I was in a pinch for cash and borrowed heavily from some individual investors. After that, things got out of hand."

"Loan sharks," John said flatly. "They always find a way of making you pay and pay."

And suddenly Daniel recalled the two men he and Stephanie had encountered in Dominic's office.

"I didn't know they were shady. And even if I had, I was so desperate for the cash, I would have agreed to any amount of interest. The problem came when I couldn't repay them fast enough and they began pressuring me, threatening to hurt Alice and the children."

Daniel slid down into a chair. Hell. His brother was in deep trouble. If he hadn't been so focused on his new business and in pursuing Stephanie, maybe he would have noticed in time to help. "Why? You're well-heeled. Why would you be in a pinch?"

"You don't understand," Dominic said miserably. "When the economy began to flounder my company cut back. I was one of the higher salaries, so I was expendable. And with the new baby coming and Jeffrey entering university, Alice spent more and more. I couldn't bring myself to tell her that I'd been sacked. She's always expected the best. She wouldn't understand."

Yes, Dominic's wife was quite a spender and, though Daniel hated to think it, she was a self-centered social climber who might not stand by her man in a financial crisis. Not like Stephanie, who didn't care how much money Daniel invested or how much he gave away. She'd liked him—correction: loved him—for who he was.

A sharp pain stabbed through his heart, cutting off his air. He couldn't think about Stephanie. He was here to help his brother. With concerted effort, he focused in on the terse conversation between John and Dominic.

"So working here wasn't a means of getting acquainted with the family?"

"I'm sorry, John. It wasn't. This job was all I had."

John leaned forward in the chair, elbows on knees, fingers steepled out in front of him. Intense emotion, whether anger or disappointment Daniel couldn't say, radiated off him. "So you set up false service accounts and embezzled money from your own family?"

Daniel tried to read John's face. What was going on behind their father's tired eyes? What would he do with this information? Was he the kind of man who could send his own son to prison?

Daniel clenched his fists. Probably. But he'd have to do it over Daniel's dead body.

"I'll pay the money back. I swear." Dominic's voice was hoarse with desperation.

"This is a huge sum, Dominic. The restaurant is in serious jeopardy because of the losses. We have little choice. We must take action and we must do it now."

Daniel leaped from his chair, jaw tight, blood rushing to his head. "I'll repay the money myself, but I won't see my brother in prison."

He could cancel the furniture. As much as asking for favors would grind against him, he would even cancel the office lease and ask John for a small office space in one of the restaurants.

Energized by the hope that he could help, he spun toward Dominic. "I have a little savings put back and my company is under way. I can borrow against it."

"Absolutely not!" John's reaction thundered through the room. He rose and moved to stand next to Dominic, clasping a hand upon his son's shoulder. "I'm your father. Helping you is my place, not your brother's."

Dominic's mouth fell open. "Sir? Are you serious?"

Daniel had the same reaction, staring in speechless bewilderment. Was the man serious?

Jaw set in determination, John nodded. "When you were small lads, I wasn't there. And I regret every day and every year that I missed. I never had a chance to buy you a bicycle or your first car. I never bought your school uniforms or paid for your food or took you to a football match." His voice dropped as he studied Dominic's face. "Don't you understand, son? I need to be the one to see you through this difficulty. No matter how great the expense, I will find a way to cover the loss."

All the air went out of Daniel. Deep inside, in that place that had been frozen for so long, a layer of hurt and anger melted away. Was this what family was supposed to be? Was this what he'd shut out of his life for so long?

John had every right to be furious and to call the police. But instead, he behaved as if—as if—he cared. He behaved like a loving father.

Dominic, as stunned as Daniel, slowly rose from his desk chair. "Sir. I don't know what to say. I'm grateful beyond words."

Moisture glinted in John's eyes. "I don't want gratitude. I want my sons."

In that instance, Daniel watched a weight of worry lift from his brother as he experienced for the first time the healing power of a father's love.

His own chest expanded to the point of bursting. He, who hadn't cried since grammar school, blinked back tears.

Maybe family was a good thing after all.

Forty-five minutes later, still reeling from the scene in Dominic's office, Daniel finished packing his business materials in preparation for the move. He'd promised to have dinner with the family at John's house later tonight. The idea that he looked forward to an evening with his father no longer surprised him. Stephanie was right. John was a good man. Daniel felt privileged to have that good man's blood running through his veins.

Regret pulled at him. He'd realized something else, too. He wasn't half the man his father was. Unlike John, he'd let someone down in her hour of need. When Stephanie had needed him most to help her through the loss of her only parent, he'd walked away.

"Nice guy, Stephens," he muttered.

Maybe he should call her, apologize. See if she was all right. Make sure her ex hadn't discovered her return to Colorado.

He gnawed on the idea, all the while jamming items in boxes. Somewhere in this mess of papers was a number she'd left in case the restaurant needed her. A tiny smile tugged the corner of his mouth. Stephanie would have a fit if she could see the mess he'd made of her flat.

The telephone jangled. He dropped a handful of files into a box before answering.

"Stephens International Water Design."

After a momentary pause such as is common to overseas transmission, a very feminine American voice spoke. “Oh, hello. Is that you, Daniel?”

“It is. Who’s this?” He balanced the receiver between chin and shoulder and went on packing.

“Rebecca Valentine. Well, Rebecca Tucker now. Your first cousin, I believe?”

Rebecca. Another relative that he had never met. But Stephanie spoke fondly of his uncle Robert’s oldest daughter, and they chatted regularly by telephone.

“Rebecca. Hello, then. How’s married life?” Stephanie had talked with excitement about her friend’s unexpected romance with a Wyoming rancher. He’d even seen some wedding photos.

A soft laugh danced over the long-distance wires. “Wonderful. There’s nothing like love to slap you up-side the head and make you look at life in a whole new way.”

Talk of love made him uncomfortable, especially considering the crazy thoughts he was having lately.

“If you’re calling for Stephanie, I’m afraid you’ve missed her. She’s in Colorado.”

This time the pause was pregnant. “You’re kidding.”

He wished. “She left a few days ago. Her father passed on, and she had to go back to settle the estate.”

“Not alone. Promise me she didn’t go alone.”

The stab of guilt was all too real. “She did.”

“Oh, but that’s horrible, Daniel. Someone should be with her. She shouldn’t have to face that house alone.”

Cold fingers of dread crawled up his spine. “That house? What do you mean?”

“Something terrible happened to Stephanie in that

house. I just know it. She never talked about it. You know how she is. Very private, almost secretive about her past. But she said enough for me to guess that her father may have abused her. She despised him and she despised that house."

"But I thought…" His stomach rolled in revulsion as the truth hit him. He'd blamed the ex-boyfriend when all along the scars, her fears, her nightmares, all stemmed from whatever had happened to her in the family home in Colorado. She was that little girl, the victim of abuse. "Oh, no."

She hadn't begged him to go with her out of grief for the loss of her father. She'd been afraid to face the past alone.

"I am a fool," he breathed. "I should have gone with her."

"Go now, Daniel." Rebecca's voice deepened with emotion. "If you care about her, please go. She needs you. Go."

She needed him, in much the way Dominic had needed John. And, heaven help him, he needed her, too. His very bones cried out for her and he'd been too blindly wrapped in self-preservation and selfishness to realize the truth.

If he cared, Rebecca had said. Oh, he cared all right. He loved her. Daniel Stephens, man without a heart, loved the strongest, most amazing woman on earth.

He sank to his knees amidst the mess of papers on the living-room floor. As soon as he could breathe again, he was going to America.

CHAPTER TEN

SHE couldn't do it.

Stephanie lay on the bed in her room at the Adam's Mark Hotel. The room had grown too cool, but she hadn't the energy to get up and adjust the heat. Outside the window a soft snow fell, pure and white and silent.

Fully dressed in a turquoise and black ski sweater, black pants and boots, she had readied everything needed to make the trip out to the suburbs. The portfolio of legal papers. Telephone numbers to call. She'd even contacted the auction house to sell off Randolph's extensive art collection and her mother's collection of antiques. They were prepared to begin cataloging as soon she could let them into the house.

Until the house was cleared of all furnishings and personal belongings, she couldn't leave Colorado. But after a few days of watching the Weather Channel she still hadn't mustered the courage to drive out to Littleton.

Randolph's final, hideous attack on her emotions had taken a toll. Immersed in a depression unlike anything she'd ever experienced, she wondered if her mother's mental fragility was a part of her internal makeup, too.

She squeezed her eyes tightly shut, only to find her mother's haunted eyes and Randolph's mocking smile behind her eyelids.

"You killed my mother," she whispered. "I won't let you kill me, too."

With every bit of effort she had, Stephanie tried to rise from the bed.

Halfway up, she dropped back with a sigh. Maybe tomorrow would be better.

Turning on her side, she stared out the window at the drifting snowflakes.

When her room phone rang, she jumped. For a nanosecond, her foolish heart hoped the caller might be Daniel. But she knew better. Daniel was gone from the Bella Lucia flat by now, and that was for the best. He would have turned away from her eventually anyway. Better now than later.

More likely the call was her attorney, urging her to get on with it. She let it ring into silence.

Five minutes later, someone tapped at her door.

"Who is it?" She wasn't in the mood for housekeeping.

"Open the door and see for yourself."

Her heart slammed against her ribcage. Only one man possessed that purring burr in the back of his throat. "Daniel?"

Here? In Colorado?

What could he want? Had something happened in London?

Her stomach twisted into a knot. No matter what his reasons for coming, seeing him was going to hurt. And she just couldn't take any more of that today.

Trepidatiously, she opened the door.

At the sight of him, big and dark and all man, she felt her knees wobble and the ache of love she wanted to escape rose up like a tidal wave.

"Why are you here?" Darn her voice for quivering. She blocked his entrance. No way was he coming into this room.

Daniel had different ideas. Gently, he pushed inside and closed the door behind him. "I made a terrible mistake and I want you to forgive me."

Stephanie crossed her arms protectively and turned away, going to the window. She felt him, all six feet four and muscles, move pantherlike up behind her.

Eyes squeezed tight, she prayed he wouldn't touch her. She'd crumble like a dry cracker if he did.

He didn't. And she was both relieved and disappointed.

"Stephanie. I've come across the ocean to find you. Hear me out."

A snowflake the size of a silver dollar swirled like an autumn leaf in front of the window. She focused on it. Cold, fragile, dying.

"You were right all along. I do have the ability to love. You taught me that. Maybe I'm not all that lovable, but I believe you love me. I've just endured four plane changes and six thousand kilometers without sleep to tell you that—" he paused and the air pulsed between them "—I love you."

Not now. Please not now. She'd spent almost a week coming to grips with the fact that the breakup was inevitable and for the best.

Feeling colder than death, Stephanie rubbed her

hands up and down the soft mohair sleeves. Her father's voice yelled inside her head. "Worthless. Bad seed. If he knew the real you, if he saw the scars, he wouldn't be here."

Better to leave the break in place and move on than to chance rejection again when he discovered her ugliness.

"No, Daniel. You were right. It's over between us."

"Don't do this, Stephanie." He sounded as ragged as she felt and so desperate, she hurt for him. "I beg you. I know I made a mistake. I know I hurt you. But please don't give up on something as good as what we have."

"You can't love me, Daniel. It won't ever work."

"Why?" he whispered and moved closer.

"Because you don't really know me. The real me. If you did, you'd run back to London."

He touched her shoulder, tugged gently at the loose, stretchy neck of her sweater.

Horror tore like a whip down her back. She dipped away, pushing at his hand. "Don't."

But Daniel proved relentless.

With a tenderness that melted her resistance, he pulled the neck of her sweater down just enough to reveal the crisscross of flayed, damaged shoulder.

Afraid of the revulsion she would see, Stephanie couldn't look at him. Blood rushed to her head, pounding, swishing, pressing until she thought she would faint. Shame filled her.

"Look at me," his beloved voice demanded. "I love you, Stephanie. I love you. All of you."

"I'm so ashamed," she whispered, her voice raw and thick with the need to cry.

When she didn't look up, Daniel forced her chin up with his opposite hand. She felt humiliated, shamed, and afraid; tears filled her eyes. She shook her head and tried to pull away.

"Don't hide from me, love. I know. I saw." Head bent so the dark, unruly locks of hair tickled the side of her neck, Daniel kissed her shoulder.

"And you can still say you love me?"

"I love you even more. Your strength. Your courage. A man who didn't appreciate you would be a fool. I've been a fool."

A dam burst inside her then. With a sob, she fell against him. His two powerful arms caught her up, kissing her face, her tears, her hair; murmuring all the words she'd longed to hear.

After the first fierce storm had passed, Stephanie pulled away. Drawing in a shuddering breath, she asked, "Do you want to know?"

Daniel took the question as a test. She had to know if he would balk now, when the worst was yet to come.

Determined not to blow this chance to prove his love, he kept his gaze steady and sure, his eyes not leaving hers as he led her to the bed.

He was scared out of his wits to know the horror she'd been through. But he loved her. And he wanted to be strong enough to carry her pain so she could let it go.

He lay down, then pulled her down beside him. She stretched out, full-length, staring up at the ceiling.

Daniel leaned up on an elbow to look down into her aqua eyes and told her about the day he'd come into the flat and seen the scars. Then, he said, "Tell me what happened."

She studied his face for the longest time. He could read all the fears, the worries, the doubts that telling the story held for her. But gradually the wall of wariness slipped away and was replaced by trust. She trusted him. At last. And in the power of that realization, his love grew tenfold.

"I loved my mother," she said simply. "She was kind and sweet, but emotionally fragile. I blame Randolph for that."

"Your father?"

She shook her head and red hair fanned out over the white pillow. "No. Thank goodness. He was my stepfather, though I didn't know until I was nine years old. That day I came home from school and heard them arguing. My father was browbeating Mother as he always did in his snide, cruel, controlling way. He called her a whore. I'll never forget how awful the word sounded, though I barely understood its meaning."

"What were they arguing about?"

"Me, it turns out. Mother thought he was too strict, too harsh. And he was. He would punish me for the least thing. A book left lying on the table. A spot of dirt on my dress." Her gaze glued to the ceiling as if she watched a movie overhead. "The night before he'd whipped me with his belt because I couldn't remember the title of a painting."

"All this time I thought your ex—" He slid down to lie beside her, hiding the horror he felt.

She shook her head. "No. Brett did hurt me, but not

that way. He couldn't handle my past. And I was afraid you'd be the same."

"Oh, my sweet." With an arm around her back, he rolled her towards him. Tremors rippled through her, tearing at Daniel's self-control. "You've carried this burden alone for too long. The man must have been a maniac."

"Yes, he was. But only Mother and I knew. He was so smooth, a politician, a social success. He took pride in parading his possessions, especially his collection of the great masters, before company. My job was to recite the names and artists in his vast repertoire. Heaven help me if I forgot one."

Daniel fought to stay silent though he wanted to rage at the evil man who'd hurt her so. Randolph Ellison had scarred more than her body. He'd scarred her soul.

"He'd always told me I was bad and worthless. That was why he punished me so much. I could never understand why he didn't love his own daughter. That day, he brought all my mother's sins out to throw them in her face. She'd had an affair, got pregnant with me, and Randolph used that indiscretion to control her—and me—for the rest of her life."

Now Daniel understood her obsessive tidiness. Keeping things in order gave her a sense of control. The more anxious she became, the more she needed the environment around her under control.

"How did he know you weren't his child?"

She gave a small, sad laugh that was no laugh at all. The warmth of her breath soughed against the skin on his neck.

"The great and mighty Randolph Ellison was sterile.

An accident of some kind when he was a boy. He and Mother had never planned to have children."

"Surprise, surprise," he said softly.

"From what little she told me, he didn't seem angry at first. He'd told her they would pretend the child was his and no one would ever know. That was the way Randolph worked. His revenge knew no bounds, but he wanted to punish her slowly and completely. And that's what he did. Over the years, he picked away at her self-esteem, convincing her that she couldn't survive without him. He controlled her every movement, her social life, everything. She grew depressed and nervous, an emotional wreck until she had a breakdown. After that, I had to protect her, too. She was so fragile."

"Couldn't she have gone to your real father for help?"

She pressed one hand against his chest as if he was her lifeline. The urge to protect her hit him like a freight train.

"He was married, too."

"What a nightmare." He twined one of her curls around the end of his finger, calming the storm inside with the repetitive action. He'd be no good to Stephanie at all if he let go of the building rage.

"My finding out the truth infuriated Randolph. He didn't have to hold back his hatred anymore. That's when the real beatings began."

Daniel had seen the ritualistic scars. She didn't need to describe the torture for him to know what had happened.

"What about your mother?"

Stephanie swallowed hard. Her voice fell to a sad whisper. "She overdosed on antidepressants when I was seventeen. I still feel so guilty about that."

"You? Why? Your stepfather was the one who drove her to it."

"She was upset because of me. She'd tried to interfere during one of his…" Stephanie's voice trailed off. She stared out the window, unable to go on. Daniel wasn't sure he could bear to hear anymore.

"I understand, love. No need to elaborate." He stroked her hair over and over, offering the only comfort he could. "Why didn't you tell someone? Why didn't anyone stop him?"

"I tried to tell once. But Randolph was a very smart, very powerful man. He knew how to work the system to his benefit. No one believed the fabulous, charismatic attorney would ever do such a thing. I was branded a spoiled, lying child. And after he finished with me that time, I was afraid to ever tell again."

"So you kept the abuse inside all these years."

"Except for Brett. And that was a disaster. He was horrified, revolted by the scars and abuse. I felt ugly, untouchable." Her voice dropped. "Unlovable."

"He was an idiot. You are the most beautiful, incredibly lovable woman in the world."

She smiled, a tremulous, teary smile that broke his heart. And he felt such joy to know he could love someone this way.

"After Brett, I gave up on love for good."

"Not for good. I'm here now. And you will not give up on me. I won't allow it."

"What changed your mind?" she asked, stroking a hand over his bewhiskered face. He'd had the devil of a time getting here and no time to shave.

"You."

She raised an eyebrow.

"You haunted me. I couldn't sleep. And then something happened that woke me up to the power of loving someone." He told her about John's reaction to Dominic's embezzlement.

"So it *was* Dom. Oh, Daniel, I'm so sorry."

He was sorry ,too, but didn't want Stephanie to see how worried he was. "John seems set on seeing him through this."

"He will. Your father is both powerful and decent, a rare combination."

"Yes, I'm sorry for all the times I resisted getting to know him. My mum had poisoned our minds about him." But Stephanie already knew about his troubled relationship with his mother. No need to go through that again.

Tugging on a lock of her hair, he aligned her body with his. "Enough about them," he whispered against her soft, lush lips. "Let's talk about us."

"Is there an us?"

"Absolutely."

With a happy sigh of surrender, he lost himself in the pleasures of her sweet mouth. She responded so sweetly, so passionately that he was hard-pressed to break away.

"I have to ask you something."

"Mmm," she murmured dreamily, tracing his lower lip with one finger.

"You're distracting me, woman."

"My intention."

He grabbed her finger and kissed it, then held her hand prisoner against his chest. "Will you marry me?

Will you put up with this moody Englishman who has nothing to offer except the promise that I'll spend the rest of my life giving you all that I am and all that I have?"

He loved the way her eyes, so sad moments before, sparkled now. He loved the way her face softened with happiness. He loved everything about his Stephanie.

"Well?" he persisted.

"When?"

"What do you mean, when?"

"When do you want to get married?"

"This afternoon."

She laughed. "This afternoon? Daniel! A girl has to plan."

He heaved a beleaguered sigh. "Okay. I'll give you a week."

"After the estate is settled. I don't want that or anything else to spoil our wedding day."

Yes, getting that painful experience behind her was necessary to her peace of mind as well as his.

"Deal. I'll help you get things settled. Meanwhile make your plans, because you are going to be my bride as soon as possible." He rolled to a sitting position and reached for the phone. "Let's call London. After the week he's had, I think my father could use a little good news, don't you?"

Smiling her answer, his beautiful bride-to-be sat up, too, wrapped her arms around his waist and gazed up at him with an expression that made him believe he could conquer the world.

Drawing her against his side where he always wanted

her to be, he connected with the overseas operator and waited until he heard his father's voice.

"Hullo?" he said.

"Daniel? Son? Is that you?"

"Yes, Dad. It's me." And the joy that burst in his chest at finally saying that simple word erased the years he'd been a fatherless son.

CHAPTER ELEVEN

HE WAS whistling in the shower.

Stephanie pinched her arm to be sure she wasn't dreaming. Daniel, her love, her heart, had come all the way from England to propose. Imagine that! All the way across the Atlantic to tell her of his love.

Dressed in her usual long flannel pajamas, she stood at the hotel window, watching the snow dance around the streetlights and cast a white glow in the darkness. In a matter of a few hours, she'd gone from depressed to joyous, all because of Daniel. With him at her side, she could face anything, even the task of cataloging and dispensing the contents of her childhood prison.

A deep, rumbling baritone replaced the cheery whistle.

Stephanie smiled.

He had to be exhausted, suffering from jet lag, but he'd taken her to an elegant, wonderful tea at the gracious old Brown Hotel. Over tiny finger sandwiches and Earl Grey tea, he'd told her over and over again that he loved her. They'd talked and talked until their hearts were full and their jaws aching. The burden of her disturbing responsibilities had lifted just by sharing them with him.

Afterwards, they'd walked the snowy streets of Denver to the Molly Brown House and made the trek upstairs, amused at how such a tiny nineteenth century place could have once been considered the grand house of Colorado's wealthiest citizen.

Just then, Daniel came out of the bathroom, rubbing his face with a towel.

"How's this?" he asked, rubbing her cheek with his.

"Smooth." She sniffed. "You smell good, too."

He flipped the towel over one bare shoulder. "I suppose I should have done this before going to tea."

"We would have missed it if we'd waited any longer."

"The phone call to London took more time than I expected."

Stephanie smiled. "Good news takes time to share. Speaking of London, now that Louise is back, do you think she'll invite her new family to the Christmas party to meet the Valentines?"

"Can't say. I fear I don't know Louise that well. At least, not yet."

All either of them really knew about Louise was her reputation as the kind-hearted, conservative, good daughter of John and Ivy Valentine. She'd been traveling so much lately, having only returned to England the day before Daniel had left for America, that Daniel had had no time at all to become acquainted.

Whatever Daniel was about to say next was smothered by a huge yawn, and Stephanie laughed. "I think your body must be losing its battle with jet lag."

"Are you complaining about my body?" He flexed a muscled arm.

Playfully, she squeezed his biceps and gave an exaggerated shiver of admiration. "Your physique is magnificent, as you well know, Mr Conceit. But you *are* tired."

"Yes, I am. Exceedingly." Naked chest and all, he pulled her to him for a kiss. His skin was cool and damp and fragrant with soap. "My internal clock doesn't know where I am or what time it is."

He flopped onto the bed and tugged her down. "Come here."

Her pulse stuttered. She knew he expected to spend the night, and that was fine with her. Having him here was all she really wanted. But she hadn't spent the night in the same bed with a man in a very long time.

All her old fears and anxieties flooded in. What if he changed his mind? What if he only imagined he could handle the way her body looked?

As if he understood, Daniel clicked off the lamp, leaving only the dim lights from the streets. "Just lay beside me, love. Let me hold you."

The tension in her shoulders eased. Being held by Daniel was exactly what she wanted. And she knew he loved her. He wouldn't force anything she wasn't ready for.

Glad to be covered from neck to ankle, Stephanie slid beneath the sheet and nestled against Daniel's broad chest. It felt so good to be wrapped in his embrace, protected by his strength.

His calloused hand rubbed up and over her hair, her neck, her shoulder, then drifted down to massage her back. "Did I tell you lately that I am totally, madly in love with you?"

"Not in the last two minutes."

He shifted to his side and bracketed her face with his fingertips. "I love you. You can't imagine how good it feels to be able, finally, to say that. To feel that."

"I know."

"Are you worried about tomorrow?" he asked, eyes searching hers in the semi-darkness.

She swallowed a lump of tenderness. He was so wonderfully thoughtful.

"A little." A lot. Tomorrow she had to face the house. And she was scared. "But I don't want to talk about that. Not tonight."

Today had been too special to mar with tomorrow's worries.

"Enough talk then," he murmured, and his mouth found hers.

The kiss was sweet and hot and hungry. His intention was clear. He loved her; he wanted her.

And she wanted him. The rest should come naturally. For a normal person it would. But not for her.

"Daniel," she said, plucking nervously at the collar of her pajamas. "Please don't be angry, but I'd rather wait until our wedding night."

He looked pathetically disappointed. If she hadn't been so worried, she would have laughed.

"It's just—" She hesitated, afraid to say what was on her mind. Regardless of Daniel's claim to the contrary, Stephanie had a horrible fear that, somehow, the ugliness could still drive him away.

Daniel stopped her fidgeting hands with his.

"The scars?" he asked.

She nodded.

"I've seen them, remember? And you're still beautiful to me."

The awful truth rose in her throat like a sickness. She wanted to tell him. He deserved to know.

While she hesitated, he said, "My love, if you were scarred from head to toe, I would still love you. And because I love you so much, I'll try to be patient. I'll even take another room after tonight. Just remember, though, on our wedding night—" he tugged gently at her pajama top "—this will go. All of it will go. And I will see and love all of you. There will be no more secrets between us."

Long after Daniel's magnificent chest rose and fell in exhausted slumber, Stephanie lay staring at the ceiling.

He was so sweet, so understanding. And he'd asked so little of her. She only hoped that when the time came, she would have the courage to give him what he asked.

Daniel awakened disoriented. A sliver of glare had snaked between a pair of green drapes to laser him right in the eyes.

As he rolled over memory flooded in stronger than the glare. He was in America. With Stephanie.

Contentment expanded his chest. If he didn't have such a jet-lag hangover, he might shout with happiness.

Thrusting out one hand, he searched the sheets for his lady.

"Stephanie?" His voice was a morning frog.

No answer.

He pried open one eye, saw nothing, and opened the other.

"Stephanie?" He sat up, looking, listening.

With a frown, he shoved the covers away and padded through the room. "Where are you?"

The bathroom door stood open. No Stephanie, but a yellow note was stuck to the mirror. He yanked the paper down.

Just as he'd suspected. She'd gone to the property to begin sorting through her nightmare.

"Stubborn, independent female," he muttered, then stomped around the room, grabbing clothes and shoes in a fit of temper. "No business going out there alone."

In record time he dressed, found the address, and called a taxi. Stephanie shouldn't face that house alone.

The ride to the suburbs was beautiful and the snowy scenery cooled his hot temper. The snow had stopped and sun glistened off the fields of white. Kids had ventured out to roll huge balls into snowmen. City workers in oversized machinery pushed piles of the fluffy stuff to the sides of the road.

But while his eyes admired the Mile High city, his mind recalled last night.

He'd been disappointed. What man wouldn't be? The woman he loved had been in the bed beside him all night and he hadn't been able to do more than kiss and hold her. If his body hadn't been so tired, he'd have spent the night in a cold shower.

He hated what had happened to her. And he was going to prove his love by waiting until she was ready to trust him. The scars were horrid, not because of how they looked but because of how she'd come to have them. But they truly didn't matter to him.

The taxi slid to a halt outside a gated residence. "This is it."

Daniel paid the driver and got out. He stood at the opened gate, staring down a long, curving, snowy driveway toward a mansion set upon a knoll.

What a place!

An enormous house, built of some sort of golden-red wood, cedar perhaps, rose three stories high against a backdrop of the Rocky Mountains. The fresh snow decorated the roof and shrubbery, giving the place a fairy-tale appearance. Who would believe such a stunning home could hold such an ugly secret?

He spotted her then, standing beside her silver rental car. The driver's door was open as if she'd just stepped out. One hand shading her eyes, she stared up at the house.

Daniel broke into a trot and his boots crunched at the dry snow. Before he reached her, she whipped around.

Dressed in the long black leather coat, red hair spilling around her shoulders, cheeks kissed pink by the cold, she took his breath away.

"Daniel," she said simply.

"Why didn't you wake me?" he panted, out of air from the run and the unaccustomed altitude. "I didn't want you coming here alone."

She smiled. "This morning, for the first time, I finally believed that Randolph Ellison can no longer hurt me." A peace she'd never had before emanated from her. "You did that for me, Daniel. You made me strong enough to face anything." She reached out a hand gloved in black leather, and touched his cheek. "This house is my burden to bear, not yours."

He squelched another burst of temper. If she thought for one minute he would walk away and leave her to face this house alone, she was sadly mistaken. "Call me chauvinistic, but when you agreed to marry me, your problems became mine. I'm here. And I'm staying. Get used to it."

Her smile grew brighter than the glaring snow. She threw her arms around his neck. "You look positively fierce. And you've just reminded me of why I love you so much."

She kissed him, a full, smacking kiss that made him laugh.

"Come on, then. Let's get this job done."

She turned to face the house again and Daniel saw her hesitate as some of her bravado slipped away. She really was terrified of this building.

He took her gloved hand in his. "Together, my love."

With her cheeks a little rosier than usual, her eyes a little brighter, and her face set like stone, she led him up on the porch and inside the house.

The immaculate, enormous vaulted great room looked as if the owner were only away for the day. As neat and tidy as Stephanie's flat, the furniture was uncovered, the huge stone fireplace laid with logs, and the wood floors polished to a sheen. Even the potted plants lining the foyer looked green and healthy.

"Someone has been caring for the house?" he asked.

"I discontinued the service yesterday."

"So, what's the plan today?"

"Inventory. I brought a laptop." Her voice was quieter than usual. Her eyes moved from side to side as if watching, waiting for the bogeyman to appear.

Daniel ached for her, but he didn't comment. She had to confront this symbol of her past on her own terms before she could put it behind her for good.

As they moved through the rooms he noticed the magnificent collection of paintings and sculptures decorating the lavish interior. Unlike Stephanie's thoroughly modern works, these pieces were classics, several that he was surprised to see outside of museums. Stephanie saw them, too, and her hands twisted restlessly against the slick leather of her coat. This artwork, some pieces near priceless, had cost her far more than it would ever be worth.

When they passed in front of the massive stone fireplace, Stephanie took down a photograph of a beautiful red-haired woman.

"My mother," she said simply.

He stepped up close and looked over her shoulder.

"You look like her." Right down to the haunted eyes.

"A little maybe. Randolph said I resembled my worthless father."

"Randolph, as we well know, was an unmitigated fool." Anger hovered around the edge of his words. He wished Randolph Ellison were still alive because he personally wanted to make him pay for all the harm he'd done.

Picture held tightly against her chest, Stephanie continued to roam the house, saying little, doing nothing as far as inventory. Daniel held her hand and tagged along, letting her take the lead. This was her show. He wanted to do it her way. And he'd be here for whatever she needed.

Through two dining rooms, an enormous kitchen, a sun room, a hot-tub room complete with skylight, and a massive games room, Stephanie seemed to hold up well, though she was far quieter than usual. The old familiar way she had of distancing herself from other people returned, and it was as if she knew he was there, but he wasn't.

They started up the wide spiral staircase.

"Five bedrooms up here," she said woodenly. "All with private baths. Wasn't that wasteful in a family of three?"

They looked inside each one and Daniel noticed that each had its own balcony with exterior stairs leading down to a small garden. Beyond that, a wooded acreage led into the mountains.

"What about the third floor?" he asked.

She hesitated. A pinch of white appeared around her lips. "One dormer room. Mine."

"You were up there alone?"

"Yes. With no way down but these stairs that led right past the master bedroom. He made sure I couldn't run away."

Daniel bit back an angry curse. His poor, precious little rich girl. Alone in her ivory tower prison, except for the madman downstairs.

She hesitated another second longer, contemplating the dark landing above. Then she dropped his hand, put her mother's photo on the bottom step, and started up. She looked for all the world like a condemned queen on her way to execution.

A terrible foreboding started Daniel's blood racing. Suddenly, he didn't want her up there. He could inventory and empty this part of the house.

"Stephanie?" he said, just as she pushed open a cherrywood door and stepped inside, out of his field of vision.

In the two strides he took to be inside the room, she had started to come undone. She shook violently. Her chest rose and fell in agitation.

And then Daniel understood. This had been the room of her torture, of her beatings, and God only knew what else. He had to get her out of here.

He reached for her elbow. "Sweetheart—" he started.

She jerked away.

"Why?" she asked in a voice so anguished that Daniel's knees began to shake.

"Why did you hurt me? I was just a little girl."

As if in a daze, she moved forward, trembling, whimpering. When she reached the fairy-princess bed, she fell to her knees, arms thrust forward across the white bedspread in a posture of submission.

And then she raised her head and screamed.

"I hate you. I hate you! Do you hear me, you evil monster? I hate you! I'm glad you're dead. I'm glad you're dead. You had no right to hurt me."

Daniel slid to the floor beside her but she didn't seem to know he was there. His heart said to stop her, but his gut said she needed this. Throat aching, he bit down on his fist and kept quiet.

Stephanie shook so hard the bed quaked, but still she railed on against the criminal who'd made her childhood a living hell. Sweat broke out on her face. Her eyes streamed tears. Her voice grew raw and raspy, and yet she raged.

Her total brokenness terrified him. He'd never felt so helpless.

When at last the torrent ceased, Stephanie's exhausted body went limp. Daniel gathered her to him, heart shattered in a thousand pieces with the tender concern he felt for his woman.

"Shh," he crooned. "Shh. He can't hurt you ever again. Not ever."

"Daniel?" she said, still quivering.

"I'm here, love. Everything is okay, now."

"He's dead, isn't he? He's really dead?"

"Yes, love. Yes."

"I'm glad." She looked up at him, aqua eyes red-rimmed and teary. "Oh, Daniel, am I a bad person because I'm happy that someone is dead?"

The pressure inside Daniel's chest reached breaking point. "If you're bad," he ground out, "I'm worse. I wanted him to be alive so I could have the pleasure of killing him myself."

"Daniel," she whispered, her fingers touching his cheek. "You're crying."

Crying? Him? The tidal wave of emotions, love, anger, sorrow, overwhelmed him then. Now he knew he had a heart because it was broken. For her.

He crushed her to him, rocking her back and forth. He kissed her hair, her swollen eyes, her wet cheeks, and after a while he simply held her.

He wasn't sure how long they sat there on the floor, but eventually, Stephanie stopped trembling and sat back.

"Better?" he asked.

She nodded. "Much."

And then his brave, strong woman dried his tears

and hers, and smiled. A wet, wobbly, sad effort, but still a smile.

"Let's go back to the hotel, Daniel. The nightmare is over. And I'm so very, very tired."

Three weeks and an enormous amount of work later, the last of the valuables from the mansion had been inventoried and readied for auction. Some days, after they'd done all they could with the property, Stephanie relaxed by shopping or jogging while Daniel spent hours by phone and computer doing business back in London.

The days passed, and as the remnants of her early life were catalogued and set aside Stephanie was amazed at how her inner spirit slowly healed. Confronting the memories locked in that house had freed her.

Even Thanksgiving, a holiday that normally held little meaning for her, had taken on a special significance. She'd told Daniel over a quiet dinner in the hotel, "I have you this year. For that, I will ever be thankful."

Now, as she sat on the hotel bed, up from a power nap, Stephanie sorted through the final pile of legal papers.

"I'm still not sure what to do with the house," she admitted, gnawing the end of a pencil. "I had originally planned to set it on fire and watch it burn."

Daniel, who sat at the small round hotel table perusing the newspaper, didn't seem the least troubled by that revelation.

The newspaper rustled as he lay it down. "A waste of perfectly good lumber."

"And some very costly furnishings." She pushed

the papers aside and padded to the exterior vanity. "Ugh. Bed head."

"A charming sight, I assure you." Daniel grinned, causing her heart to flip-flop. "Let me."

He took the brush and gently began the job of untangling the mass of curls. "I have a thought about the house. Are you open to suggestions?"

"From you?" She gazed up at him in the mirror. His eyes were serious. "Of course."

"The estate has a legacy of hurt. Change that. Make it a place of helping."

And as suddenly as that, an idea popped into her head.

"Daniel, that's brilliant. I know exactly what I want to do." Excitement zipped through her blood stream. "I'll call my attorney and have him investigate our options."

"For what? Tell me."

"A safe house for abused women and children. A place for them to come without fear, to heal and get on their feet. There's enough money with the estate to keep it in perpetuity."

"What a terrific idea."

"I would never have thought of it without you." She whirled around and took the brush from his hands. On tiptoe, she kissed him. "I love you. You are so smart."

"Keep talking." He walked her backward toward the bed. "On second thought, don't talk. Kiss."

With a laugh of happiness, she did exactly that as Daniel tumbled them down.

After far too much kissing that left them both frustrated, Daniel groaned, "If you want to wait until our wedding night, we'd better get married today."

"Think you can wait until Monday?"

"This coming Monday?"

He looked so wonderfully hopeful that Stephanie laughed. "Yes. Most everything I have to do is taken care of now. My mind is clear of all those stressors. And I don't want to wait any longer to be your wife."

The corners of his eyes crinkled. "I hear Aspen is beautiful this time of year."

"Aspen?" A bubble of happiness rose in her chest. "I still have friends in Aspen." But Daniel knew that already, a reminder of how thoughtful and considerate her husband would be. "It's the perfect romantic spot for a wedding, however impromptu."

He pumped his eyebrows. "And a honeymoon?"

"Yes." She jumped up, pulled him up with her, and danced them around the hotel room. "A Christmas wedding in Aspen."

Unlike Denver, Aspen held good memories and a few friends she'd kept in touch with. A phone call or two to the Snowbound Lodge could set things in motion.

And if she had any worries about the wedding night, Stephanie was too happy at the moment to think about them now.

CHAPTER TWELVE

THE bride wore Christmas green.

Daniel's stomach dipped the moment Stephanie stepped out of the chapel's tiny dressing room to join him in the short walk down the aisle. She'd warned him that her dress was not traditional, claiming she looked terrible in white. Modest cut, chic and elegant, the long emerald velvet was the perfect complement to her flowing red hair. Her mother's diamond choker and matching earrings sparkled like Christmas lights against her peach skin.

He cleared his throat, found it uncommonly dry, but managed to say, "You are beyond gorgeous."

She smiled up at him, her aqua eyes gone as green as her dress. "Wanna marry me?"

Fighting the need to crush her to him and carry her off like some barbarian, he breathed, "Oh, yeah."

He was either going to marry her or kidnap her. One way or the other, she was going to be his today. He'd waited as long as he could stand it, a notion that still astounded him. He had never expected to marry, let alone love a woman the way he loved Stephanie.

"Then lead the way, handsome man. I wanna marry you, too."

He folded her hand, soft and smooth as the velvet fabric, over his elbow and led her toward the minister waiting at the front of the chapel. Behind the clergyman, floor-to-ceiling windows offered a spectacular view of the forest, and beyond that, the snow-covered Rockies. Stephanie had chosen this quaint little chapel, nestled in the trees near Aspen, for this view. But Daniel found the vision beside him far more breathtaking.

From somewhere came the sound of a harp playing "Ave Maria", so gentle and heavenly that he felt transported by the sheer beauty of the place, the melody, the moment. One glance at Stephanie's enraptured face told him she felt the same.

When they reached the minister, a graying, middle-aged man with smile lines, the music ceased and the ceremony began. The minister read from the Bible and spoke lovely words that roared in Daniel's head like the sound of the sea rushing in. He didn't care what was said as long as the end result was the same. But Stephanie deserved a special memory and he intended for her to have it.

The ceremony seemed to go on for ever and yet be over in a moment. During the exchange of rings, Daniel's hands trembled, not with anxiety or fear, but with an emotion so powerful he thought he might go to his knees. He, a man who had braved floods and droughts and so much more was reduced to tremors by the sound of Stephanie whispering her eternal promise of love.

At last, the moment came when she was his for evermore, and, with his heart near to bursting, Daniel kissed his bride. Not once, but over and over again until all of them, minister, witnesses, and the newlyweds, were laughing.

The harp music began again and to the accompaniment of "Ode to Joy", a fitting piece if ever he heard one, Daniel and his bride completed the formalities and prepared to leave.

"I have a surprise, Mrs Stephens." Daniel draped a long fur cape over her shoulders and opened the door.

A pair of large, hairy-footed golden horses waited docilely in front of a curved white sleigh.

Stephanie gasped and looked up, expression so full of love and excitement he knew he'd made the right choice. "Daniel, I love it. I love you."

She kissed him.

"Just the reaction I was hoping for."

A sleigh ride might be clichéd, but it was exactly the kind of romantic gesture he wanted to do for her. The sleigh was only the first of several surprises he had planned for this special night…and for his special bride.

Snow kissed their faces as the driver "tsked" the horses into motion. Snuggled beneath a heavy fur lap robe, Daniel held his lady-love close. All the while, his heart was singing.

Horse hoofs thudded softly against the packed snow; harness a-jingle, they journeyed out of the pines and into town.

"Aspen is a fairy tale at Christmas," Stephanie said as the sleigh glided down Main Street.

Every building in the quaint resort of the rich and famous was bathed in lights so that the town glowed with warmth and holiday cheer. Festive green and red decorated the storefronts, the streetlamps, the windows, the doors, and, as if the human effort weren't enough, nature supplied the constant cover of snow and the backdrop of majestic mountain peaks and stunning star-sprinkled sky.

Cheek against hers, he pointed upward. "Did you see that?"

"A shooting star," she said and he could feel her smile curve upward. "We have to make a wish."

But Daniel's wishes, even the ones he hadn't known he wanted, had all come true. A father. A family. And now a wife. He gazed down at her. Her eyes were squeezed tight in the pale moonlight. "What did you wish for?"

"You already know," she murmured, opening her eyes. "I wish for us to always be as happy and in love as we are tonight."

"Your wish is hereby granted." He sealed his promise with a kiss.

They rode along in silence for a while, snuggled close sharing warmth and smiles. The scent of wood smoke from nearby homes teased the air, and an occasional car motored past. Once, they heard snatches of Christmas carols coming from a brightly lit building—a country club party, he surmised.

The cold of Colorado made Daniel's skin tingle. He used the chill as an opportunity to hold his wife a little closer.

When at long last she shivered, he said, "You're getting chilled. Maybe we should go to the cabin now."

"This is so wonderful. I hate for the night to end."

"We'll ride as long as you choose, but remember, love…" he rubbed her nose with his "…the night has only just begun."

Stephanie's skin tingled, too, though not from cold. She loved the invigorating smell and feel of cold mountain air. She tingled from the delicious suggestion in Daniel's voice, and the notion thrilled her. Even though the nagging worry about tonight didn't leave, with all her heart she wanted to be Daniel's wife in every way.

"I'm ready to go to the lodge when you are," she said and was rewarded with a heart-stopping kiss.

Daniel spoke to the sleigh driver and they began the trip away from the city proper.

When the sleigh turned north, Stephanie sat up to look around. "This isn't the way back to the lodge, is it?"

"We're not going to the lodge." Daniel's expression was smug and secretive.

"But our things are there."

"Not anymore."

A zing of excitement heated her blood. Daniel, her husband, her love, was making tonight a beautiful adventure.

The sleigh turned down a narrow, tree-lined lane and headed deeper into the woods. The horses slowed to a gentle stop in front of a small cabin, illuminated from without and within.

"Your honeymoon cottage, my love." Daniel hopped

down and playfully bowed toward the small cabin nestled in the snow-laden pines.

"It's perfect."

And it was. From the wreath on the door to the romantic interior where a small fireplace already crackled.

Inside, Daniel slid the fur cape from her shoulders and dropped it onto a stuffed chair. "This is our little hideaway for the next week."

"How did you do this? Everything was booked when I called."

"That's because I called first."

"Sneaky." She trailed her fingers over a small wooden bar where a large basket of Christmas cookies, gingerbread men and foil-wrapped chocolates awaited them. "But very wonderful. I think I might fall madly in love with you if you keep this up."

"Admit the truth. You fell for me the minute I invaded your flat."

She smiled. "Maybe I did. But you also scared me to death. Such a barbarian, all dark and wild with those big muscles."

He stalked toward her. "Are you scared now?"

"Terrified." With a squeal, she danced away from his outstretched hands, laughing. Her heart raced a little faster.

She grabbed for the cookie basket. "Want a cookie?"

His grin was absolutely feral. "Nope. I want you."

He caught the sleeve of her dress and tugged. She catapulted into his arms, stomach fluttering with excitement.

"There's hot mulled cider," she teased, knowing that neither of them was at all interested in food. At least not right now.

His eyelids drooped to a sexy stare. "I'd rather have hot married you."

Stephanie felt the heat of a blush but loved knowing that her new husband wanted her so badly.

"So impatient," she said, a complete untruth. He'd been a paragon of patience since their engagement, giving her all the time and space she needed.

"Love the way you look in this dress." He ran a finger beneath the sweetheart neckline. She shivered with the thought that soon he would see her, touch her, everywhere. "I'd love it even more if you'd take it off."

Stephanie laughed, a husky sound that surprised even her. She tugged at his tie, enjoying the mating ritual.

"And you look so handsome and sophisticated in this suit."

"Handsome? Sophisticated?" He gave her a mock frown. "What about virile? Tough? Strong?"

She struck a pose, vamping for him, her voice intentionally seductive. "Manly, rugged, and, oh, so sexy."

"Want to find out how sexy I can be?"

"Maybe." She touched the diamond choker at her throat. "Would you help me with this?"

"We have to start somewhere," he murmured wryly. Then he unclasped the necklace, whisked it from her, and replaced it with his lips. His soft whiskers tickled deliciously. Stephanie let her head fall back. A low hum vibrated from her throat to his mouth.

"Are you trying to seduce me?" she asked when she could finally speak.

"How am I doing?" he murmured against the pulse dancing wildly beneath her collarbone.

Stephanie couldn't answer. She was too busy angling her neck this way and that to capture the luscious feel of his hot mouth and tongue on every inch of her skin.

"I have earrings too," she finally managed to say, though the words were breathy.

He chuckled. "Yum."

In turn, he removed each one and suckled her earlobes, nuzzled the sensitive skin beneath her ear, kissing her until they were both breathless.

"Anything else you want removed?" he whispered, his voice a throaty purr.

She loosened his tie and in a slow, sexy dance slid it from his neck. She trailed the narrow band of silk across his face. He caught the end with his teeth in a sensuous tug-of-war.

"Maybe I should slip into something more comfortable," she said.

Eyes widening, he dropped the tie like a hot potato.

"Meet you in the bedroom in five minutes?" he asked hopefully.

A tiny knot of anxiety formed in her stomach. Even though they'd been working toward this moment for weeks, some of her playful eagerness drained away. As much as she loved this man, she dreaded the moment he would see her.

"I'm a little nervous," she admitted. Actually she was a lot nervous, but telling Daniel the truth helped. He knew and he understood that her reasons were not about him, but about herself.

"Don't be, love. Don't be." He took the tie and looped it around her neck, using the strip of cloth to pull her close, swaying them from side to side. "I love you more than I can say. And want you just as much. Nothing is going to change that."

She hoped he was right.

"I want you, too. So, so much." Gathering her courage, she kissed his jaw. "Five minutes."

When she came out of the bathroom in a robe she'd bought especially for tonight, Daniel already waited in the bed, his broad chest nude and golden in the glow of the fireplace. The overhead lights were out and only a small lamp lit the room. She silently blessed his thoughtful concession to her modesty and fear.

"We can turn out all the lights if you'd rather," he said.

"What do you want?"

"Whatever you do."

Though she knew his preference, she loved him for giving her the choice. "Leave them on."

He reached for her, but she backed away, standing in the full light from the fire. If she was going to do this with lights on, she would do it all.

Gaze locked on Daniel's face, she untied the belt of her robe and let it drop. She had to watch his reaction.

"I haven't told you everything, Daniel."

"You don't have to."

"Okay, then. I'll show you. No secrets, remember?" She let the shoulders of the satin robe slither halfway down to her elbows.

Daniel levered up to watch, his pupils large and dark in the fire-glow, the sheet falling to his trim, rippled belly.

"More than my back is scarred," she whispered.

"Let me see." His voice was soft, compassionate, loving. She could do this. For him. For herself.

She let the robe slide ever so slowly past her arms, over her hips to puddle at her feet.

She stood, naked and vulnerable, heart pounding wildly as she watched his reaction. The revulsion she expected never came.

"You…are…so…beautiful," he ground out between jaws clenched with desire.

In that moment, Stephanie knew she had found the impossible. A man who looked past the horrible scars of her childhood to the woman inside.

All her doubts and fears fell away to join the robe at her feet when Daniel's nostrils flared and his eyes darkened in passion.

"Come here, woman," he growled.

Slowly, proudly, she moved toward him, reveling in the mounting passion she evoked in her new husband. Not pity. Not revulsion or sympathy or even anger. But love and passion.

"I love you," she said as he pulled her onto the bed with him.

His body trembled against hers, and she loved him even more.

And then with an exquisite tenderness that brought tears to her eyes, Daniel laid her back against the downy pillows and gently kissed every scar on her body until she no longer thought of anything except becoming one with her forever soulmate.

* * *

Daniel awoke to the warm, delightful smell of fresh coffee. For three glorious days now, his beautiful bride had managed to awaken before him and fill the cabin with delicious smells. Tomorrow he simply had to wake up first and make her breakfast in bed.

"Morning, my love." She swept into the bedroom, carrying two steaming cups. Her face scrubbed clean and pink, her hair tied back at the neck, she looked fresh as the mountain air.

He took the mug, sipped at the warm brew, and then said, "You're interfering with my plans."

She perched on the edge of the mattress. "How so?"

"I want to do the spoiling, but you don't give me a chance."

She pushed the hair back from his forehead with one cool, soft hand and kissed him. He loved it when she did that. "Daniel, you made our wedding day—" she paused to smile "—and night perfect. You've made every day since perfect. Fixing breakfast makes me feel like a real wife. I love it."

"Do you love me, too?" He could never get enough of hearing her say it.

"Oh, a little, I suppose." She grinned, and seeing her relaxed and carefree enough to tease filled him with enormous joy.

He was still on an emotional high from their wedding night. As hard as it must have been for her, Stephanie had undressed for him—had wanted to. And by that action, his beautiful, brave wife had given him the finest wedding gift of all—her trust. No one had ever sacrificed anything for him that he remembered. But she had.

After the initial shock of seeing what her stepfather had done to her body, he'd seen only the woman he loved more than life. With his heart bursting, he'd vowed at that moment that no one would ever hurt her again, beginning with him.

"What do you want to do today?" he asked, setting his cup on the bedside table. "The world is yours. I'll even get the universe if you want it."

"I'm sorry to bring this up, but—" she ran a fingertip around the rim of her cup "—we're going to have to think about going back to London soon."

"No-o-o." He flopped backwards on the bed in protest. But he knew she was right. They both had work to do that couldn't be done long distance, but being here with Stephanie was magical. He'd never been so fulfilled.

"Louise phoned earlier."

"My sister?"

She smiled, and Daniel lifted one shoulder in response. Referring to Louise as his sister was starting to feel okay.

"Things are chaotic. Your father and Robert are arguing constantly because Robert thinks Dominic belongs in jail. John won't hear of it, of course. Money is very, very tight and there is talk of closing one or more of the restaurants. She thought we should know."

The problem, thanks to his brother, was approaching crisis state.

"I talked to Dominic yesterday. He's worried, too. As he should be, but still..." He let the rest ride. Dominic was his twin. Regardless of the mistake he'd made, Daniel would stand by him just as John was doing. In the face of such desperate odds, Daniel was amazed at their father's steadfast loyalty.

"So what do you think we should do?"

He sighed. "Book our flights."

"Agreed." She rose from the bed and set her coffee cup beside his. "But first, I have a present for you."

He pumped his eyebrows. "You're coming back to bed?"

She laughed. "Maybe. But something important came by messenger a few minutes ago, and I can't wait to share the news with you." She left the room, only to return a moment later carrying a brown envelope.

"Remember all that fabulous art my stepfather collected?"

Yes, he remembered. And he also recalled the abuse she'd suffered when she hadn't been able to remember the titles and artists. He'd wanted to tear the paintings from the wall and rip them apart with his bare hands.

She handed him a legal-looking document. "That collection auctioned for an enormous sum of money."

"Good. Are you planning to add that to your Hope House?"

She shook her head. "This document creates a trust to help fund Daniel Stephens' water projects in Africa."

Incredulous, he stared from her to the document. "You're serious. That's really what this is."

"Yes. If I'd known a crisis would arise in the family, I would have saved some out for that. But I didn't. And this is already in motion. A trust of this kind can do an enormous amount of good."

"You put your inheritance into this? For me?"

"My wedding gift to you. I know how important those projects are to you. Now they're important to me." She climbed on the bed beside him, touched his cheek with her fingertips. "You changed my life, Daniel. You made me feel beautiful and desirable and worthy. You took away my shame. Nothing I give you will ever be enough."

Love, almost more than he could contain, exploded inside him. This woman, this incredible, generous, valiant woman had taken the ugliness of her childhood and created something beautiful. And in the process, she'd changed him, an empty, heartless shell of a man.

And as he contemplated the priceless gifts Stephanie had given him—her love, her fears, and now her inheritance—Daniel let go of the bitterness he'd carried so long.

CHAPTER THIRTEEN

"IT'S a Christmas party." Over the softly crooning music of "White Christmas," Daniel spoke close to Stephanie's ear. She was understandably nervous about tonight. "What bad thing could possibly happen?"

Daniel gazed around at the gathered assembly. Seated with them at the corner table were Daniel's cousins, Rebecca and Rachel, both pregnant and with their new husbands by their sides. Across the room, Rebecca's stepchildren played wide-eyed under the Christmas tree. A host of Valentines, of whom Daniel and his bride were both now a part, swarmed the gaily decorated interior of the Bella Lucia Mayfair. Beneath the outward gaiety, the strain was almost palpable.

"A Christmas party that is also an emergency family meeting. Things could get sticky before the evening is over."

She nodded toward Robert and his wife, ensconced at one end of the room, and then toward John, who'd taken a table at the other end. The two brothers, who'd never gotten along, were really at odds now.

"This is my first ever family Christmas," Daniel said. "I think I'll enjoy myself and forget the rest." He dropped a kiss on her hair, and filled his lungs with her fresh designer fragrance. He was only telling half the truth. He was worried, too. As hard as he'd tried to remain detached from his blood relatives, they had a way of sucking him in. And now they were in trouble.

Regardless of some happy news, including Daniel and Stephanie's elopement, bad news seemed to be the order of the day. Dominic's embezzlement had caused much greater damage than John had anticipated.

Without a huge infusion of money from Lord-knew-where, the Bella Lucia chain would be bankrupt. John was striving valiantly to protect Dominic and had drained his personal accounts in the effort. Robert was furious with them both and threatening everything from lawsuit to strangulation. All involved, including Stephanie, were concerned about their livelihoods. Daniel felt guilty to see his own dreams coming true when others were losing theirs.

"You two look cozy," Rebecca said, smiling toward Daniel and Stephanie. "How was the honeymoon?"

"Perfect," they answered in unison and then burst out laughing. No one would ever know how perfect. They'd skied, hiked, and gone sledding. They'd dined out and in. They'd strolled the woods and the streets of Aspen. But mostly they'd stayed in the secluded cabin and reveled in the joy of their love.

"Did I ever thank you for sending me to America?" Daniel asked.

Rebecca reached across the table to squeeze Stephanie's arm. "Seeing my friend happy is thanks enough."

"You look pretty happy yourself," Stephanie said, returning the squeeze.

"Delirious." Suddenly, Rebecca's eyes widened. "Daniel," she said in amazement, "is that your sister?"

They all looked in the direction of Rebecca's gaze. A tall blonde in a white angora crop top and red micro mini had entered the dining room. Mistletoe jewelry flashed from her belly button. At her side was a tall, tanned fellow who probably had every woman in the place staring at him.

Daniel choked on his drink. "That's not the Louise I remember."

Gone were the classic designer suits, subtle makeup and hairstyle. Miss Goody-Two-Shoes looked red-hot.

"We're not the only ones noticing her new look." Stephanie hitched her chin toward Max. Daniel's cousin, who helped Robert run the Bella Lucia Chelsea, glowered at the outrageously clad Louise and her escort.

"Don't mind Max," Rachel said. "The two of them have never gotten along."

"Hmm. I wonder." Rebecca's eyes sparkled beneath the white blinking Christmas lights. "Sometimes all that fighting is a mating dance."

Mitchell, Rebecca's husband, chuckled indulgently. "I'm afraid you'll have to overlook my wife. She sees romance everywhere these days."

Rebecca grinned up at him. "You complaining?"

He hooked an elbow around her neck and pulled, his besotted expression clear to all. "Nope."

"Romance or not, Louise is here for the same reason

we are. Because this family has big problems." Rachel seemed set on fretting. And rightly so. She'd been a favorite of Grandfather William's and had invested her adult life in these restaurants. "I, for one, don't know what we're going to do."

"I've offered to take a cut in salary," Stephanie said. "Others have done the same."

"The business needs a lot more money than salary cuts can generate. Unless Uncle John and Dad come up with a plan soon, the entire chain will have to close. But the way those two quarrel, I can't see that happening."

"Surely, they can find an investor, Rachel. Doesn't anyone in this huge family have that kind of money?"

"There is one. But he won't help."

"Who's that?"

"Jack. Dad's other son, my other half brother, the estranged one. But he washed his hands of this place and all the Valentines a long time ago."

Odd. Daniel had never heard of this cousin. "Will he be here tonight?"

"Are you kidding?" Rachel shook her head. "Jack hasn't been to a family gathering in years. He hates this place. All the others may put aside their differences at Christmas, but not Jack. If this place sinks, he'd be the last person on earth to throw out a life-preserver."

Above the lilt of "Have Yourself a Merry Little Christmas" came the tinkle of metal against glass. Soon the room took up the chorus of tapping and conversation hushed.

John rose. His face was drawn and weary, his usual ruddy vigor gone, and Daniel thought with a start that his father looked old. He'd had a mild heart attack a few months back and now the strain of Dominic's misdeed was taking a heavy toll.

Still, he carried himself erect, and, with a determined set to his chin, he started across the room toward Robert.

"I would like to propose a toast," he said. The sound carried among the assembly now gone quiet except for the soft Christmas carols playing through the sound system. All eyes watched as John approached his brother's table.

Robert looked startled; an inward struggle played across his features. Finally, as if he had no choice, he rose, wineglass in hand. The rest of the crowd rose as well.

"Tonight," John said, his gaze intent on the other man's face, "is Christmas. All of us are here because we're family. If only for this one night, let's forget our problems, and celebrate all the good things that have happened to us this year." When Robert didn't protest, he went on, gathering momentum. "Here is a toast to all of us. Young and old. Old and new. We face some challenges, but the indomitable spirit of the Valentine family will prevail. Somehow, some way, we will prevail. May the coming year bring happiness, peace, and prosperity to us all."

"Hear, hear," someone in the crowd called. And a chorus of the toasts rose and fell. Glasses clinked.

Daniel used that diversion as an excuse to maneuver his bride beneath a sprig of mistletoe. "Merry Christmas, wife."

"Merry Christmas, husband," she said as his smiling lips melded with hers.

When the kiss ended and the clinks and good wishes faded away, the front door of the restaurant, closed to all but family, whooshed open. Cold December air flooded in.

The party, wineglasses held high, turned as one to see who the latecomers were.

A collective gasp emptied the room of oxygen.

For there in the doorway stood Madison Ford, Jack Valentine's assistant. And next to her, a cynical half-smile on his face, was none other than the prodigal son himself, Jack Valentine.

0806 Gen Std HB

SEPTEMBER 2006 HARDBACK TITLES

ROMANCE™

Purchased for Revenge *Julia James*	0 263 19230 X
The Playboy Boss's Chosen Bride *Emma Darcy*	0 263 19231 8
Hollywood Husband, Contract Wife *Jane Porter*	0 263 19232 6
Bedded by the Desert King *Susan Stephens*	0 263 19233 4
A Mistress for the Taking *Annie West*	0 263 19234 2
The Pregnancy Secret *Maggie Cox*	0 263 19235 0
The Bejewelled Bride *Lee Wilkinson*	0 263 19236 9
Bought for Marriage *Margaret Mayo*	0 263 19237 7
Her Christmas Wedding Wish *Judy Christenberry*	0 263 19238 5
Married under the Mistletoe *Linda Goodnight*	0 263 19239 3
Snowbound Reunion *Barbara McMahon*	0 263 19240 7
The Tycoon's Instant Family *Caroline Anderson*	0 263 19241 5
Plain Jane's Prince Charming *Melissa McClone*	0 263 19242 3
Project: Parenthood *Trish Wylie*	0 263 19243 1
Her Miracle Baby *Fiona Lowe*	0 263 19244 X
The Doctor's Longed-For Bride *Judy Campbell*	0 263 19245 8

HISTORICAL ROMANCE™

A Lady of Rare Quality *Anne Ashley*	0 263 19054 4
Talk of the Ton *Mary Nichols*	0 263 19055 2
The Norman's Bride *Terri Brisbin*	0 263 19056 0

MEDICAL ROMANCE™

The Christmas Marriage Rescue *Sarah Morgan*	0 263 19094 3
Their Christmas Dream Come True *Kate Hardy*	0 263 19095 1
A Mother in the Making *Emily Forbes*	0 263 19513 9
The Doctor's Christmas Proposal *Laura Iding*	0 263 19514 7

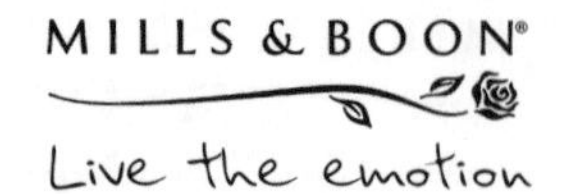

0806 Gen Std LP

SEPTEMBER 2006 LARGE PRINT TITLES

ROMANCE™

The Greek's Chosen Wife *Lynne Graham*	0 263 18998 8
Jack Riordan's Baby *Anne Mather*	0 263 18999 6
The Sheikh's Disobedient Bride *Jane Porter*	0 263 19000 5
Wife Against Her Will *Sara Craven*	0 263 19001 3
The Cattle Baron's Bride *Margaret Way*	0 263 19002 1
The Cinderella Factor *Sophie Weston*	0 263 19003 X
Claiming His Family *Barbara Hannay*	0 263 19004 8
Wife and Mother Wanted *Nicola Marsh*	0 263 19005 6

HISTORICAL ROMANCE™

A Practical Mistress *Mary Brendan*	0 263 18915 5
The Missing Heir *Gail Ranstrom*	0 263 18916 3
The Gladiator's Honour *Michelle Styles*	0 263 19074 9

MEDICAL ROMANCE™

His Secret Love-Child *Marion Lennox*	0 263 18883 3
Her Honourable Playboy *Kate Hardy*	0 263 18884 1
The Surgeon's Pregnancy Surprise *Laura MacDonald*	0 263 18885 X
In His Loving Care *Jennifer Taylor*	0 263 18886 8
High-Altitude Doctor *Sarah Morgan*	0 263 19523 6
A French Doctor at Abbeyfields *Abigail Gordon*	0 263 19524 4

0906 Gen Std HB

OCTOBER 2006 HARDBACK TITLES

ROMANCE™

The Christmas Bride *Penny Jordan* 0 263 19246 6
Reluctant Mistress, Blackmailed Wife *Lynne Graham* 0 263 19247 4
At the Greek Tycoon's Pleasure *Cathy Williams* 0 263 19248 2
The Virgin's Price *Melanie Milburne* 0 263 19249 0
The French Count's Pregnant Bride *Catherine Spencer* 0 263 19250 4
The Billionaire's Marriage Mission *Helen Brooks* 0 263 19251 2
The Christmas Night Miracle *Carole Mortimer* 0 263 19252 0
The Millionaire's Reward *Angie Ray* 0 263 19253 9
The Bride of Montefalco *Rebecca Winters* 0 263 19254 7
Crazy About the Boss *Teresa Southwick* 0 263 19255 5
Claiming the Cattleman's Heart *Barbara Hannay* 0 263 19256 3
Blind-Date Marriage *Fiona Harper* 0 263 19257 1
A Vow to Keep *Cara Colter* 0 263 19258 X
Inherited: Baby *Nicola Marsh* 0 263 19259 8
A Father By Christmas *Meredith Webber* 0 263 19260 1
A Mother for His Baby *Leah Martyn* 0 263 19261 X

HISTORICAL ROMANCE™

An Improper Companion *Anne Herries* 0 263 19057 9
The Viscount *Lyn Stone* 0 263 19058 7
The Vagabond Duchess *Claire Thornton* 0 263 19059 5

MEDICAL ROMANCE™

The Midwife's Christmas Miracle *Sarah Morgan* 0 263 19096 X
One Night To Wed *Alison Roberts* 0 263 19097 8
A Very Special Proposal *Josie Metcalfe* 0 263 19515 5
The Surgeon's Meant-To-Be Bride *Amy Andrews* 0 263 19516 3

0906 Gen Std LP

OCTOBER 2006 LARGE PRINT TITLES

ROMANCE™

Title	Author	ISBN
Prince of the Desert	*Penny Jordan*	0 263 19006 4
For Pleasure...Or Marriage?	*Julia James*	0 263 19007 2
The Italian's Price	*Diana Hamilton*	0 263 19008 0
The Jet-Set Seduction	*Sandra Field*	0 263 19009 9
Her Outback Protector	*Margaret Way*	0 263 19010 2
The Sheikh's Secret	*Barbara McMahon*	0 263 19011 0
A Woman Worth Loving	*Jackie Braun*	0 263 19012 9
Her Ready-Made Family	*Jessica Hart*	0 263 19013 7

HISTORICAL ROMANCE™

Title	Author	ISBN
The Rogue's Kiss	*Emily Bascom*	0 263 18917 1
A Treacherous Proposition	*Patricia Frances Rowell*	0 263 18918 X
Rowan's Revenge	*June Francis*	0 263 19075 7

MEDICAL ROMANCE™

Title	Author	ISBN
The Doctor's Unexpected Proposal	*Alison Roberts*	0 263 18887 6
The Doctor's Surprise Bride	*Fiona McArthur*	0 263 18888 4
A Knight to Hold on to	*Lucy Clark*	0 263 18889 2
Her Boss and Protector	*Joanna Neil*	0 263 18890 6
The Surgeon's Convenient Fiancée	*Rebecca Lang*	0 263 19525 2
The Surgeon's Marriage Rescue	*Leah Martyn*	0 263 19526 0